W9-ADI-024

Some Kind of Wonderful

**Center Point
Large Print**

Some Kind of Wonderful

DEBBIE MACOMBER

CENTER POINT PUBLISHING
THORNDIKE, MAINE

This Center Point Large Print edition
is published in the year 2007 by arrangement with
Harlequin Enterprises, Ltd.

The text of this Large Print edition is unabridged. In other
aspects, this book may vary from the original edition. Printed in
Thailand. Set in 16-point Times New Roman type.

ISBN-10: 1-60285-042-9
ISBN-13: 978-1-60285-042-2

Library of Congress Cataloging-in-Publication Data

Macomber, Debbie.
    Some kind of wonderful / Debbie Macomber.--Center Point large print ed.
    p. cm.
    ISBN-13: 978-1-60285-042-2 (lib. bdg. : alk. paper)
    1. Large type books. I. Title.

PS3563.A2364S595 2007
813'.54--dc22

2007012697

To Dale Wayne Macomber,
who claims his mother never dedicates anything
to him.

What are little boys made of: Snails? Puppy
dogs' tails? Nope. Twelve-year-old boys are
made of football cards, dirty socks stuffed in a
drawer, mag bicycle wheels and stealing preteen
girls' hearts.

1/08

Chapter One

"Once upon a time in a land far away," Judy Lovin quoted in a still, reverent voice. The intent faces of the four-year-olds gathered at her feet stared up at her with wide-eyed curiosity. Hardly a whisper could be heard above her soft enunciation as Judy continued relating the fairy tale that had stirred her heart from the moment she'd first heard it as a youngster no older than these. It was the story of Beauty and the Beast.

Today, however, her thoughts weren't on the fairy tale, which she could recite from memory. As much as she'd tried to focus her attention on her job, Judy couldn't. She'd argued with her father earlier that morning and the angry exchange had greatly troubled her. To disagree with her father, a man she deeply loved and respected, was rare indeed. Charles Lovin was an outspoken, opinionated man who headed one of the world's most successful shipping companies. At the office he was regarded as a tyrant—demanding, but fair. At home, with his family, Charles Lovin was a kind and generous father to both Judy and her older brother, David.

Charles's Wedgwood teacup had clattered sharply when he'd placed it in the saucer that morning. "All those years of the best schooling and you prefer to work as a preschool teacher in a day-care center." He'd said it as though she were toiling among the lepers on a South Pacific island instead of the peaceful upper east side of Manhattan.

"I love what I do."

"You could have any job you wanted!" he'd flared.

His unprovoked outburst surprised Judy and she'd answered quietly. "I have exactly the job I do want."

His hand slapped the table, startling her. Such behavior was uncommon—indeed, unheard of—in the Lovin household. Even her brother couldn't disguise his shock.

"What good are my wealth and position to you there?" he roared. "Beauty, please . . ."

He used his affectionate name for her. She'd loved the fairy tale so much as a child that her father had given her the name of the princess in the timeless tale she'd read repeatedly. Today, however, she felt more like a servant than royalty. She couldn't recall a time when her father had looked at her in such a dictatorial manner. Swallowing a sip of tea, she took her time answering, hoping to divert the confrontation.

She was a gentle soul, like her mother, who had died unexpectedly when Judy was in her early teens. The relationship between father and daughter had grown warm and generous in the years that followed and even during her most rebellious teen years, Judy had rarely argued with him. And certainly not over something as trivial as her employment. When she'd graduated from the finest university in the country at the top of her class, she'd gone to work as a volunteer at a local day-care center in a poor section of town.

She'd come to love her time with these precious preschoolers. Charles hadn't objected then, or when she'd been asked to join the staff full-time. Her pay was only a fraction of what she could make in any other job. After all these months, it seemed unfair that her father should object now.

"Father," she said, keeping calm. "Why are you concerned about the day-care center now?"

He'd looked tired and drawn out and so unlike himself that she'd immediately grown concerned.

"I'd assumed," he shouted, his expression angry, "that given time, you'd come to your senses!"

Judy attempted to disguise a smile.

"I don't find this subject the least bit amusing, young lady."

"Yes, Father."

"You have a degree from the finest learning institution this country has to offer. I expect you to use the brain the good Lord gave you and make something decent of yourself."

"Yes, Father."

"Try living off what you make taking care of other women's children and see how far you can get in this world."

She touched the edges of her mouth with her linen napkin and motioned with her head to Bently, who promptly removed her plate. The English butler had been with the family since long before Judy had been born. The servant gave her a sympathetic look. "Do we need the money, Father?" she asked quietly.

In retrospect, she realized she probably shouldn't have spoken in such a flippant tone. But to hear her father, it was as though they were about to be deported to the poorhouse or wherever it was people went when they became suddenly and unexpectedly destitute.

Charles Lovin completely lost his temper at that, hitting the table so forcefully that his spoon shot into the air and hit the crystal chandelier with a loud clatter startling them both.

"I demand that you resign today." And with that, he tossed his napkin onto his plate and stormed from the room.

Judy sat for a long moment as the shock settled over her. Gradually the numbness subsided and she pushed back her George II-style chair. All the furniture in the Lovin home had been in the family for generations. Many considered this a priceless antique; Judy considered it a dining-room chair.

Bently appeared then, a crisp linen towel folded over his forearm. He did so love ceremony. "I'm sure he didn't mean that, Miss." He spoke out of the corner of his mouth, barely moving his lips. It had always amused Judy that Bently could talk this way and she assumed he'd acquired his talent from years of directing help during dinner parties and other formal gatherings.

"Thank you, Bently," she said, grinning. "I'm sure you're right."

He winked then and Judy returned the gesture. By

the time she arrived at the day-care center, she had put the thought of resigning out of her mind. Tonight when she returned home, her father would be his loving, kind self again. He would apologize for his outrageous temper tantrum and she would willingly forgive him.

"Miss Judy, Miss Judy!" Tammi, a lively youngster, jumped to her feet and effectively cut into Judy's thoughts. The four-year-old threw her arms around her teacher's neck and squeezed with all her might.

"That's a beautiful story."

Judy returned the whole-hearted hug. "I love it, too."

"Did Beauty and the Beast love each other forever and ever?"

"Oh, yes."

"Did they have lots of little beasts?"

"I'm sure they did, but remember that the Beast wasn't a beast any longer."

"Beauty's love turned him into a handsome prince," Jennifer exclaimed, exceedingly proud of herself.

Bobby, a blond preschooler with pale blue eyes, folded his arms across his chest and looked grim. "Do you know any stories about policemen? That's what I want to be when I grow up."

Judy affectionately rumpled the little boy's hair. "I'll see if I can find a story just for you tomorrow."

The youngster gifted her with a wide smile, and curtly nodded his head. "Good thing. A man can get tired of mushy stories."

"Now," Judy said, setting the book aside. "It's time to do some finger painting."

A chorus of cheers rose from the small group and they scurried to the tables and chairs. Judy stood and reached above her head to the tall cupboards for the necessary equipment.

"You know what I loved most about the Beast?" Jennifer said, lagging behind.

"What was that?" Judy withdrew an apron from the top shelf and tied it around her trim waist. Her brown hair fell in gentle curves, brushing the tops of her shoulders, and she pushed it back.

"I loved the way Beauty brought summer into the Beast's forest."

"It was her kindness and gentleness that accomplished that," Judy reminded the little girl.

"And her love," Jennifer added, sighing.

"And her love," Judy repeated.

"I have the report you requested."

John McFarland glanced up from the accounting sheets he was studying. "Put it here." He pointed to the corner of his beech desk and waited until his business manager, Avery Anderson, had left the room before reaching for the thick manila folder.

McFarland opened it, stared at the picture of the lovely brown-eyed woman that rested on the top and arched his brows appreciatively. Judy Lovin. He'd seen her pictures in the society pages of the *New York Times* several months ago, but the photo had done her fragile beauty little justice. As he recalled, the article had told about her efforts in a day-care center. He studied her photograph. She was lovely, but there were far more beautiful women in the world. However, few of them revealed such trusting innocence and subtle grace. The women he dealt with possessed seductive beauty, but were shockingly short of any heart. Seeing Judy's photograph, McFarland was struck anew at the sharp contrast.

He continued to stare at the picture. Her doelike, dark brown eyes smiled back at him and McFarland wondered, for all that sweetness, if she had half the backbone her father possessed. The thought of the man caused his mouth to tighten with an odd mixture of admiration and displeasure. He had liked Charles Lovin when he'd first met him, and had been openly challenged by him later. Few men had the courage to tangle with McFarland, but the older man was stubborn, tenacious, ill-tempered . . . and, unfortunately, a fool. A pity, McFarland mused, that anyone would allow pride to stand in the way of common sense. The U.S. shipping business had been swiftly losing ground for over a decade. Others had seen it and diversified or sold out. If McFarland hadn't bought them outright, he'd taken control by other channels. Charles Lovin, and only Lovin, had steadfastly refused to relinquish his business, to his own detriment, it seemed, McFarland mused. Apparently, leaving a dead and dying company to his beloved son, David, was far more important than giving him nothing.

McFarland's gaze hardened. Lovin was the last holdout. The others had crumpled easily enough, giving in when McFarland had applied pressure in varying degrees. Miraculously, Lovin had managed to keep his company. Word from the grapevine was that the older man had been cashing in stocks, bonds and anything else he could liquidate. Next, he supposed it would be priceless family heirlooms. It was a shame, but he experienced little sympathy for the proud man. McFarland was determined to own Lovin Shipping Lines and one stubborn old man wouldn't stand in his way. It was a pity, though; Lovin had guts and McFarland admired the man's tenacity.

Leafing through the report, he noted that Lovin had managed to take out a sizable loan from a New York bank. Satisfied, McFarland nodded and his lips twisted with wry humor. He was a major stockholder of that financial institution and several other Manhattan banks as well. He pushed the buzzer on his desk and Avery appeared, standing stiffly in front of the desk.

"You called, sir?"

"Sit down, Avery." McFarland motioned with his hand to an imposing leather wing chair. Avery had been with McFarland four years and he'd come to respect the other man's keen mind.

"Did you read the report?"

"Yes."

McFarland nodded, and absently flipped through the pages.

"It seems David Lovin is well thought of in New York circles," Avery added. "Serious, hard-working. Wealth doesn't appear to have spoiled the Lovin children."

"David?" McFarland repeated, surprised that he'd been so preoccupied that he'd missed something.

"The young man who will inherit the Lovin fortune."

"Yes, of course." McFarland had examined the Lovin girl's photograph and had been so taken with her that he hadn't gone on to read what was reported about her older brother. He did so now and was impressed with the young man's credentials.

"Many believe that if Lovin Shipping Lines can hold on for another year . . ."

"Yes, yes." McFarland knew all that. Congress was said to be considering new laws that would aid the faltering U.S. shipping business. McFarland was counting on the same legislation himself.

"Father and son are doing everything possible to manage until Washington makes a move."

"It's a shame," McFarland murmured, almost inaudibly.

"What's a shame?" Avery leaned forward to better hear his employer.

"To call in his loan."

"You're going to do it?"

McFarland studied his employee, amazed that the other man would openly reveal his disapproval. It wasn't often he was able to read Andersen's thoughts.

To all the world, it would seem that McFarland was without conscience, without scruples, without heart. He was all those things and none of them. McFarland was an entity unto himself. People didn't know him because he refused to let anyone close. He had his faults, McFarland was the first to admit that, but he'd never cheated any man. His honesty couldn't be faulted . . . only his ethics.

He stood abruptly, placed his hands behind his back and paced the area in front of his desk. David Lovin was a fortunate man to have a heritage so richly blessed; McFarland knew nothing of his family. Orphaned at an early age, he'd been given up for adoption. No family had ever wanted him and he'd been raised in a long series of foster homes—some better than others.

McFarland had clawed his way to the top an inch at a time. He'd gotten a scholarship to college, started his first company at nineteen and been a millionaire by age twenty-one. At thirty-six, he was the one of the wealthiest men in the world. Surprisingly, money meant little to McFarland. He enjoyed the riches he'd accumulated, the island, his home, his Lear jet; money brought him whatever he desired. But wealth and position were only the byproducts of success. Unlike those who had allowed their fortunes to become their all, McFarland's empire would die with him. The thought was a sobering one. Money had given him everything he'd ever wanted, but it couldn't give him what he yearned for most—love, acceptance, self-worth. A paradox, he realized somewhat sadly. Over the years, he'd grown hard. Bitter, too, he supposed. Everything in him demanded that he topple Lovin as he had a hundred other family businesses. Without regret. Without sentiment. The only thing stopping him was that damnable pride he'd recognized in Charles Lovin's eyes. The man was a slugger and he hated to take him down without giving the old boy a fighting chance.

"Sir, do you wish to think this matter through?"

McFarland had nearly forgotten Avery's presence. He nodded abruptly and the other man stood and quietly left the room.

Opening the doors that led to the veranda, McFarland stepped outside, braced his hands against the wrought-iron rail and looked out on the clear blue waves crashing against the shore far below. He'd purchased this Caribbean island three years earlier and named it St. Steven's Island. It granted him privacy and security. Several families still inhabited the far side of the island, and McFarland allowed them to continue living there. They were a gentle people and he'd never had a problem with any of them. On the rare occasions when he happened to meet the inhabitants, they ran from him in fear.

A brisk wind blew off the water, carrying with it the scent of seaweed. Briefly, he tasted salt on his tongue. Farther down the beach, he saw a lazy trail of foam that had left its mark on the sand, meandering without purpose into the distance. Sometimes that was the way McFarland thought of his life; he was without purpose and yet dominated by it. Another paradox, he mused, not unhappily, not really caring.

Unexpectedly, the decision came to him and he returned to his desk, again ringing for his assistant.

Avery was punctual as usual. "Sir?"

McFarland sat in his chair, rocked back and thoughtfully fingered his chin. "I've made a decision."

Avery nodded, reaching for his paper and pen. McFarland hesitated. "I wonder how much that business means to that old man."

"By all accounts—everything."

McFarland grinned. "Then we shall see."

"Sir?"

"Contact Lovin as soon as possible and give him an ultimatum. Either I'll call in the loan—immediately—or he can send his daughter to me." He picked up the file. "I believe her name is Judy . . . yes, here it is. Judy."

Avery's pad dropped to the carpet. Flustered, he reached for the paper, and in the process lost his pen, which rolled under McFarland's desk. Hastily, he retrieved them both and, with nervous, jerky movements, reclaimed his place. "Sir, I'm . . . convinced I misunderstood you."

"Your hearing is fine."

"But . . . sir?"

"Naturally there will be several guarantees on my part. We can discuss those at a later date."

18

"Sir, such a . . . why, it's unheard of . . . I mean no man in his right mind . . ."

"I agree it's a bit unorthodox."

"A . . . bit, but surely . . . sir?" Avery stuttered, his jaw opening and closing like a fish out of water.

Watching, McFarland found him highly amusing. The man had turned three shades of red, each one deeper and richer than the one before. A full minute passed and he'd opened his mouth twice, closed it an equal number of times and opened it again. Yet he said nothing.

"What of the young lady? She may have a few objections," Avery managed finally.

"I'm confident that she will."

"But . . ."

"We'll keep her busy with whatever it is women like to do these days. I suppose she could redecorate the downstairs. When I tire of her, I'll set her free. Don't look so concerned, Avery. I've yet to allow my baser instincts to control me."

"Sir, I didn't mean to imply . . . it's just that . . ."

"I understand." McFarland was growing bored with this. "Let me know when he gives you his decision."

"Right away, sir." But he looked as if he would have preferred a trip to the dentist's office.

Judy returned home from work that afternoon, weary in both body and spirit. She smiled at Bently, who took her coat and purse from her.

"Is my father home?" Judy asked, eager to settle

19

this matter between them. If he felt as strongly as he had that morning about her job at the day-care center, then she would do as he requested.

"Mr. Lovin is still at the office, Miss Judy."

Judy checked her watch, surprised that her father was this late. He was almost always home an hour or so before her. "I'll wait for him in the study," Judy said. Something was worrying him; Judy was sure of it. Now that she'd given pause, several matters didn't set right. Whatever the problem was, Judy yearned to assure him that she'd help him in any way possible. If it meant her leaving the day-care center then she would, without hesitation, but she was happy working with the children. Surely he wanted her happiness. Being a success shouldn't be judged by how much money one happened to make. Contentment was the most important factor and she was sure that someone as wise and considerate as her father would agree.

"In the study, miss? Very good. Shall I bring you tea?"

"That would be lovely. Thank you."

He bowed slightly and turned away.

Judy entered the library, which was connected to her father's study by huge sliding doors. She chose to wait among the leather-bound volumes and settled into the soft armchair, slipped off her pumps and placed her feet on the ottoman, crossing them at the ankles. The portrait of her mother, hanging over the marble fireplace, smiled down on her. Sometimes, when Judy had been much younger, she'd thought that Georgia Lovin could actually see her from that portrait. Judy would sometimes sneak into the room and talk with her mother. On occasion, she could have sworn, Georgia's eyes had moved. That was silly, of course, and Judy had long ago accepted that her mother was gone and the portrait was exactly that—a likeness of a lovely woman and nothing more.

Judy stared up at her now. "I can't imagine what got into Father this morning."

The soft, loving eyes appeared to caress Judy and plead with her to be patient.

"I've never known him to be in such an unreasonable and foul mood."

Her mother's look asked her to be more understanding and Judy quickly looked away. "All right, all right," she grumbled. "I'll be more patient."

Bently entered the study, carrying a silver tray. "Shall I pour?"

"I'll do it," she answered him with a smile, dismissing him. She reached for the pot. "Bently?"

"Yes, miss?" He turned back to her.

"Whatever happened to the Riordan sculpture that was on Father's desk?" The small bronze statue had been a prized piece that her father had loved. It had been on top of his desk for years.

Surprise rounded the butler's aged eyes. "I'm . . . not quite sure, miss."

"Did Father move it to his office?"

"That must be it."

"He'd never sell it." Judy was convinced of that. The Alice Riordan original had been a Christmas gift from her mother a few months before she died.

"I'm sure he didn't." The butler concurred and excused himself.

Now that she thought about it, there were other items missing from the house—a vase here and there; a painting that had disappeared. Judy hadn't given the matter much thought, but now she found it odd. Either her father had moved them to another location for safekeeping or they'd simply vanished into thin air. Even to entertain the notion that the staff would steal from the family was unthinkable. Bently, Cook and Anne had been with the Lovins for years.

Judy poured her tea and added a squeeze of fresh lemon. Bently had been thoughtful enough to bring two extra cups so that when her father and David arrived, she could pour for them.

She must have drifted off to sleep because the next thing Judy heard was the sound of gruff male voices. The door between the two rooms had been closed, but the raised impatient voices of her father and brother could be heard as effectively as if they were in the same room with her.

Judy sat upright and rubbed the stiffness from the back of her neck. She rotated her shoulders, intent on interrupting her father and brother and cajoling them into a cup of tea, but something held her back. Perhaps it was the emotion she heard in their voices—the

22

anger; the outrage, the frustration. Judy paid little attention to business matters. The shipping line was her brother and father's domain, but it was apparent even to her that something was dreadfully wrong.

"You can't mean that you actually sold the Riordan?" David's astonished voice echoed off the paneled walls.

"Do you think I wanted to?" Charles Lovin returned, and the agony revealed in his voice nearly caused her heart to stop. "I was desperate for the money."

"But, Father . . ."

"You can't say anything to me that I haven't told myself a thousand times."

"What else?" David sounded worried and grim.

"Everything I could."

The announcement was followed by a shocked gasp, but Judy didn't know if it had sounded from her throat or her brother's.

"Everything?" David repeated, his voice choked. "As much as humanly possible, without losing this house . . . and still it wasn't enough."

"What about Bently and the others?"

"They'll have to be let go."

"But, Father . . ."

"There's no other way," he cried. "As it is, we're still millions short."

Judy didn't know what was happening, but this had to be some mind-bending nightmare. Reality could never be this cruel. Her father was selling everything they owned. In addition to this estate, they owned homes all over the world. There were securities, bonds, properties, investments . . . Their family wealth went back for generations.

A fist slammed against the desk. "Why would McFarland call in the loan?"

"Who knows why that beast would do anything? He's ruined better men than I."

"For what reason?"

Her father paused. "Perhaps he enjoys it. God knows, I've been enough of a challenge for him. From everything I've been able to learn about the man, he has no conscience. He's a nobody; an orphan. I doubt that he had a mother. I've owned horses with better pedigrees than McFarland," he said bitterly. The next words were smothered, as though her father had buried his face in his hands. ". . . something I didn't tell you . . . something you should know . . . McFarland wants our Beauty."

"What?" David's shocked exclamation followed.

Judy bolted upright, her back rigid. It was apparent that neither her father nor David were aware she was in the other room.

"I heard from his business manager today. Avery Andersen spoke for McFarland and stated that either we come up with the amount of the loan plus the accumulated interest or send Judy to St. Steven's."

"St. Steven's?"

"That's the name of his private island."

"What does he want with . . . her?"

"Only God knows." The agony in her father's voice ripped at Judy's heart. "He swears he won't abuse her in any way, and that she'll have free run of the island, but . . ."

"Oh, Lord." David must have slumped into a chair. "So you were left to decide between a business that has been in our family for four generations and your daughter?"

"Those were exactly my choices."

"What . . . did you tell him?"

"You don't want to hear what I said to that man."

"No," David whispered, "I don't suppose I do."

"We have no option," Charles Lovin said through gritted teeth. "McFarland wins. I won't have Judy subjected to that beast." Heavy despair coated his words.

Numb, her whole body trembling, Judy leaned against the chair. Lovingly she ran her hand over the soft brown leather. This chair, like so much of what they owned, had been a part of a heritage that had been in their family for generations. Soon it would all be lost to them.

And only she could prevent it from happening.

Chapter Two

Judy's hand tightened around the suitcase handle as she stood on the deserted dock. The powerboat that had brought her to St. Steven's roared away behind her. She refused to look back, afraid that if she did, her courage would abandon her.

The island was a tropical paradise—blue skies, gentle breezes, virgin beaches and crystal clear water. Huge palm trees bordered the beach, swaying gently. The light scent of magnolias and orchids wafted invitingly toward her.

A tall man Judy guessed to be in his late forties purposefully approached her. He wore a crisp black suit that revealed the width of his muscular shoulders. His steps made deep indentations in the wet sand.

She'd only brought one suitcase, packing light with the prayer that her stay would be a short one. The single piece of luggage now felt ten times heavier than when she had left New York that morning.

Her father had driven her to the airport, where McFarland's private jet awaited her to take her to a secluded air strip. From there she was told it would be a short boat trip to the island. Tears had glistened in his faded blue eyes. He'd hardly spoken and when the moment came for Judy to leave, he'd hugged her so tightly she hadn't been able to breathe.

"Goodbye, Judy." His whispered words had been strangled by emotions. "If he hurts you . . ."

"He won't," she assured him and gently brushed the hair from his temple. "I'll be fine—and back home so soon you won't even know I've been gone."

A pinched, aged look had come over her father then and he'd whispered, "I'll know. Every minute you're away, I'll know."

Leaving her family hadn't been an easy task for Judy, especially when she felt as though she was being ripped from their arms.

After innocently eavesdropping on her father and David's conversation, Judy had openly confronted them. She would go to McFarland and they could do nothing to stop her. Her stubborn determination had stunned them both. She had refused to hear their arguments and had simply gone about packing. Within twenty-four hours she was on her way to St. Steven's.

She was here now, outwardly calm at least, and mentally prepared to do whatever she must.

"Miss Lovin?" The man asked politely, meeting her at the end of the pier.

Judy nodded, momentarily unable to find her voice.

"We've been expecting you." He reached for her suitcase, taking it from her hand. "Come this way, please."

Like a puppet on a string, Judy followed the muscle-bound stranger. He led her into the forest of trees to a waiting cart that reminded her of something she'd seen on the golf course. Only this one was far more powerful and surged ahead at the turn of a key.

When they came upon the house, Judy's breath became trapped within her lungs. The home was the most magnificent place she'd ever seen. It had been built on the edge of a cliff, nestled in foliage, and was adorned with Roman-style pillars and huge doors. Random clusters of tropical vines climbed the exterior walls, twisting their skeletal fingers upward.

"This way," the man said, standing on the walkway that led into the grand house.

Bemused, Judy climbed out of the cart and followed him through the massive doors. In the marble entryway she was met by a short, thin man. She identified him almost immediately as McFarland's assistant—the man she'd heard her father mention. He looked like an Avery—efficient, intelligent . . . bookish.

"Miss Lovin," he greeted her with an embarrassed smile. "I trust your journey was a pleasant one."

"Most pleasant." She returned his smile, although her knees felt like tapioca pudding. "You must be Mr. Andersen."

If he was surprised that she knew his name, he didn't reveal it. "Your rooms are ready if you'd like to freshen up before dinner."

"Please."

He rang a bell and a maid appeared as though by magic. The woman's gaze didn't meet Judy's as she silently escorted her up the stairs. The maid held open a pair of double doors that led to a parlorlike room complete with fireplace, television, bookshelves and two sofas. Off the parlor was a bedroom so lovely Judy stared in amazement at the lush blend of pastel colors. The view of the ocean from the balcony was magnificent. She stood at the railing, the wind whipping her hair about her face, and saw both a swimming pool and a tennis court. To her far right, she located another building that she assumed must be the stables. Her heart gladdened. She'd been riding almost from the time she could walk and thoroughly loved horses. Her cage was indeed a gilded one.

"Dinner will be in fifteen minutes," the maid informed her softly, speaking for the first time.

"Thank you," Judy answered formally. She squared her shoulders and her heart pounded faster. Soon she would be meeting the infamous McFarland—the man her father called the Beast.

But Judy was wrong. When she descended the stairs, armed with questions, to which she was determined to find the answers, she learned to her dismay, that she would be dining alone.

Mr. Andersen lived in a small house on the island and had departed for the day. McFarland had sent his regrets, but business prevailed. His brief note indicated he was looking forward to meeting her in the morning.

The dining-room table was set for eight with a service of the finest bone china. The butler seated Judy at the far end. The servants brought in one course after another, their footsteps echoing sharply in the silent chamber. Each course was delectable, but Judy ate little. Afterward, she returned to her room.

Her sleep was fitful as questions interrupted her dreams, each demanding an answer. Judy, unfortunately, had been given none. She wondered if McFarland was playing some kind of psychological game meant to intimidate her. If he was, then she had fallen an unwilling victim to his devilish plot. She knew little about McFarland—not even his given name. He was rarely seen in public and she had been unable to locate any pictures of him. Her father insisted he was arrogant, impudent, insolent, unorthodox and perhaps the worst insult—beastly.

What a strange place this was, she thought tiredly, staring up at the darkened ceiling. The house was built in a paradise of sun and sea and yet she felt a chill pervade her bones. It wasn't until early morning that she realized there was no joy here—no laughter, no fun.

By six, she couldn't bear to stay in bed any longer. Tossing back the covers, she rose and decided to head for the stables. She yearned to ride, to exorcise the fears that plagued her.

The house was like a tomb—silent, somber and gray—as Judy crept down the stairs. The front door opened without a problem and she slipped outside. The sun was rising, cloaking the island in golden threads of light.

A noise behind her caused her to twist around. A stranger on horseback was approaching her slowly. Even from a distance, Judy noticed that he sat tall in the saddle. A cowboy hat was pulled low over his eyes.

She hesitated. No doubt he was a security guard and from the way he regarded her, he either was looking for trouble or expecting it.

"Good morning," she called out tentatively.

He touched the brim of his hat in silent greeting. "Is there a problem?" His voice was deep and resonant.

"No . . . problem? Of course not."

His finely shaped mouth curved with amusement as he studied her from head to foot. A crooked grin slashed his handsome mouth.

Not knowing what else to do, Judy returned his look, staring back at those compelling blue eyes. She thought for a moment that he was silently laughing at her and she knotted her fists. Heated color worked its way up her neck, invading her cheeks. "It's a beautiful morning."

"Were you thinking of going for a walk?" He shifted his weight in the saddle and at the sound of creaking leather, Judy realized that he was dismounting. He took a step toward her, advancing in a pantherlike tread with inherent male power.

Before she was able to stop herself, Judy stepped backward in retreat. "No . . . I was heading for the stables. McFarland said I was to go anyplace I wanted on the island and . . . I thought I'd have someone choose a horse for me. Of course, I could saddle it myself."

Bold blue eyes looked straight into her startled, round ones. "I frighten you?"

"No . . . that's ridiculous." She felt like a stuttering fool. He didn't frighten her as much as he enthralled her. He radiated a dark energy with brooding eyes and the tall, lean build.

He grinned at her response and the movement crinkled the lines around his eyes, creasing his bronzed cheeks. "Relax, I'm not going to pounce on you."

She stiffened. "I didn't think for a moment that you would." Surely the help respected McFarland's guests—if she could call herself that.

"I'll walk you to the stables." He reached for the reins and the huge black stallion followed obediently behind them.

"Have you been on the island long?" she managed shakily, and attempted to smile.

"Three years."

She nodded, clenching her hands tightly together in front of her. This was the first person she had the opportunity to speak with and she was curious to find out as much as she could about McFarland before actually meeting him. In her mind she'd conjured up several pictures, none of them pleasant. She knew he had to be an unhappy, lonely man. Old, decrepit, cantankerous. "What's he like?"

"Who?"

"McFarland."

A muscle worked in his lean jaw and when he looked at her again, his eyes were dark and enigmatic. "Some say he's the devil incarnate."

Judy grinned and lowered her gaze to the ground. "My father calls him the beast."

"The beast," he repeated, seeming to find that amusing. "Some claim there's no compassion in him. Others insist he has no conscience, and still more believe he has no heart."

She glanced at the man's lathered, dusty horse and then at him. Pride shouted in the tilt of his strong chin and the set of his shoulders. Thoughtfully, she shook her head. "No," she said slowly, "I don't agree with that."

"You don't?"

"No," she repeated confidently. "He appreciates beauty too much. And if he didn't have a conscience he would have . . ." She hesitated for a second, and realized she was saying much more than she should to a mere security guard. McFarland could have ruined her father ten times over, but hadn't. The tycoon may not have a heart of gold, but he wasn't without conscience. Nor was he cruel.

"What do you think he's like? I take it you haven't met the man."

"I'm not sure how I feel about him. As you say, we haven't met, but from what I've seen, I'd guess that there's precious little joy in his life."

The man laughed outright. "Look around you," he said and snickered. "He's said to be one of the richest men in the world. How could any man have so much and not be happy?"

"Joy comes from within," she explained softly.

"There's too much bitterness in him to have experienced true contentment."

"And who are you? Sigmund Freud?"

It was Judy's turn to laugh and she realized that she'd grown more at ease with this dark stranger. "No. I formed several opinions before I came to the island."

"Wait until you meet him, then. You may be pleasantly surprised."

"Perhaps." But Judy sincerely doubted it.

They arrived at the stables and were met by a burly fellow who ambled out to greet them.

"Good morning, Sam."

" 'Morning," the other man grumbled, eyeing Judy curiously.

"Saddle Princess for Miss Lovin and see to it that Midnight is given extra oats. He deserves it after the ride I gave him this morning."

Judy turned abruptly. "How did you know my name?"

He ignored her, but his eyes softened slightly at her bemused, questioning look. "Tomorrow, saddle both horses at five-thirty. Miss Lovin and I will be riding together."

"Consider it done, Mr. McFarland."

Red-hot embarrassment washed over Judy. She dared not look at him.

"I'll see you at lunch, Miss Lovin."

It was all she could do to nod.

The morning passed with surprising speed. It had been months since Judy had last ridden and her body was unaccustomed to the rigors of the saddle. She hadn't gone far, preferring to investigate the island another day. A hot breakfast awaited her after she'd showered and she ate greedily. When she'd finished, she had written her father a long letter, then realized there was no place she could mail it. Presently, she lay back on the velvet sofa and closed her eyes, listening to music. The balcony doors were open and the fresh sea air swirled around her.

Someone knocked politely at her door. A maid had been sent to inform Judy that lunch would be served in ten minutes.

Experiencing both dread and excitement at once, Judy stood, repaired the damage to her hair and makeup and slowly descended the stairs. She paused at the bottom, gathered her resolve and painted a smile on her face, briefly wondering how long it would be before it cracked. She didn't expect to keep the cheerful facade long, but it was important to give McFarland the impression that she had been unruffled by their earlier encounter. She clasped her hands together and realized her palms were already damp in anticipation of the second meeting with the man who ruled an empire from this island.

He stood when she entered the dining room and recognized the determination in her eyes.

"I trust your morning was satisfactory," he said in polite, crisp tones.

Boldly, Judy met his probing gaze. "Why am I here?" She hadn't meant to hurl questions at him the instant she joined him, but his discerning look had unnerved her.

"I believe it's to eat lunch. Please sit down, Miss Lovin. I, for one, am hungry, and our meal will be served as soon as you're comfortable."

The butler held out the chair at the end of the table where she'd eaten the night before. With rebellion boiling in her blood, Judy sat on the brocade cushion of the mahogany chair.

A bowl of consommé was placed in front of her. When Judy lifted her spoon, she discovered that her hand was trembling and she tightened her grip.

"How long do you plan to keep me here against my will?" she said. Six place settings separated them; the distance could have been a football field for all the notice McFarland gave her.

"You'll be free to go shortly," he announced between courses, leaving her to wait a full five minutes before responding.

"I may leave?" She couldn't have been more surprised. "When?"

"Soon." He gauged her expression grimly. "Are you so miserable?"

"No," she admitted, smoothing the linen napkin across her lap. "The island is lovely."

"Good." His eyes gentled.

"Why do you hate my father?"

The question appeared to surprise him. "I don't. I find Charles Lovin to be a man of high moral character and principle."

Judy measured his words. "You like him then?"

"Let's say I respect him."

She hated to think what McFarland would do to a man he despised.

"Whose decision was it for you to come?" he asked unexpectedly.

"Mine."

He nodded and seemed to approve. "I imagine that your father and brother were opposed to your willingness to sacrifice yourself." He said this with more than a hint of sarcasm.

"Adamantly. I probably would never have been told of your . . . ultimatum, but I accidentally overheard them discussing it."

"You were wise to have come."

"How's that?"

"I wouldn't have hesitated to call in the loan."

"I don't doubt that for a second," she returned heatedly, disliking him. Her fingers gripped the smooth napkin in her lap, but that was the only outward sign of anger that she allowed herself.

His grin lacked amusement. "If you had refused, you'd have been burdened with a terrible guilt. In time, your peace and happiness would have been greatly affected."

The butler took away her untouched salad and served the main course. Judy stared down at the thin slices of roast beef, smothered in gravy and mushrooms, and knew she wouldn't be able to eat.

"Have you always been this dictatorial?" Judy demanded.

"Always." He sliced his meat slowly.

She thought of the class of four-year-olds she'd left behind. "You must have been one hell of a child." His teen years didn't bear contemplating.

Slowly, deliberately, McFarland lowered his knife and fork to the table. His eyes grew sober. "I was never a child."

Princess was saddled and ready for her early the following morning. Judy patted the horse's nose and produced a carrot from the hip pocket of her jeans.

"At great personal danger, I sneaked into the kitchen and got you this," she whispered, running her hand down the mare's brown face. "Now don't you dare tell Sam, or he'll box my ears." It hadn't taken Judy long to realize that Sam ruled the stables like his own castle and she could well be traipsing on the older man's toes.

"Do you have something for me as well?" The deep male voice spoke from behind her.

Judy whirled around to face McFarland. "No," she said, shaking her head. "I hope you don't mind . . ." She eyed the rapidly disappearing carrot.

He was dressed in black this morning, his expression brooding. Once again his hat brim shadowed his face. His mood was as dark and dangerous as his outfit. "You needn't worry about stealing vegetables."

Without another word, he mounted his horse with supple ease, causing the leather to creak and give with his weight. He hesitated long enough to reach for the reins and sent Judy a look that stated she was welcome to join him or go her own way.

Quickly, Judy placed her foot in the stirrup and swung her lithe frame onto Princess's back, grabbed the reins and cantered after him.

McFarland rode like the very devil, leading her deep into the jungle. The footpath was narrow and steep. Birds cawed angrily and flew out of their way, their wings beating against the underbrush. Leaves and branches slapped at Judy's face; mud spattered her boots and jeans. Still he didn't lessen the furious pace. It demanded all Judy's skill just to keep up with him. She barely managed. By the time he slowed, she was winded and her posterior was sorely bruised. He directed Midnight onto the beach and Judy gratefully followed, allowing Princess to trot along the sandy shoreline.

Judy stared at him. Panting, she was far too breathless to speak coherently. "Good—grief, McFarland—do you always tear—through the jungle like that?"

"No." He didn't look at her. "I wanted to see how well you rode."

"And?"

"Admirably well." he grinned, and his eyes sparkled with dry humor. Judy found herself involuntarily returning his smile.

"Next time," she said between breathless gasps, "I choose the route." Dark mud dotted her clothes and face. Her hair fell in wet tendrils around her cheeks and she felt as though they'd galloped through a swamp.

He, on the other hand, had barely splattered his shiny boots.

"Tell me about Judy Lovin," he demanded unexpectedly as they trotted side by side.

"On one condition. I want you to answer something for me."

"One question?"

"Only one," she promised, and raised her right hand as though giving an oath.

"All right."

She granted him a soft smile. "What do you want to know?"

"Details."

"All right," she said and nodded curtly. "I weighed just under seven pounds when I was born . . ."

"Perhaps current information would be more appropriate," he cut in.

Judy threw back her head and laughed. "All right. I'm twenty-four . . ."

"That old?"

She glowered at him. "How am I supposed to tell you anything if you keep interrupting?"

"Go on."

"Thank you," she muttered sarcastically. "Let me see—I suppose you want the vitals. I'm five five, short, I know, and I weigh about . . . No." She cast a look from the corner of her eye and slowly shook her head. "I don't think that's information a woman should give to a man."

He chuckled and Judy drew back on the reins, surprised at the deep rich sound of his amusement. His laugh was rusty, as if he didn't often give in to the urge.

He gave her an odd, half-accusing look. "Is something wrong?"

"No," she responded and shook her head, feeling self-conscious. He really should laugh more often, she thought. He looked young and carefree and less— she couldn't find the word—driven, she decided.

"What about men?"

"Men?"

"As in beaux, dating, courtship—that kind of thing."

"I date frequently." That was only a slight misrepresentation of the truth.

"Anyone special?"

"No—unless you consider Bobby; he's four and could steal my heart with a pout." She stopped Princess, swung her leg over the horse's back and slowly lowered her feet to the ground.

McFarland dismounted as well.

"My turn."

He shrugged. "Fire away."

"Your name." She thought it ridiculous that a man would be called McFarland—nothing less, nothing more.

"My name? You know that."

"I want to know your first name."

"Most people don't ask."

"I'm asking."

He hesitated long enough for her to become uneasy. "It's John."

She dropped her gaze to her mud-coated boots, testing the name on her tongue.

"Well?" he prompted, silently laughing at her. "Do you think it suits me?"

"It fits," she told him, her eyes serious.

"I'm glad to hear it," he said, mocking her.

"May I call you that?"

It seemed a lifetime passed before he finally answered. "If you wish."

"Thank you," she said humbly, and meant it. "You know, you really aren't a beast."

He frowned at that and brushed a wet strand of hair from her cheek. His fingers trailed across her face, causing the pit of her stomach to lurch at the unexpected contact.

"And you, my dear, are no Beauty."

Judy went cold, halting abruptly. "How did you know my father called me that?"

"I know everything there is about you. Right down to that Milquetoast you thought yourself in love with a couple of years back. What was his name again? Richard. Yes, Richard. I am also aware that you've rarely dated since—disillusionment, I suppose."

Judy felt the blood drain from her face.

"I know you fancy yourself a madonna of sorts to that group of four-year-olds. How very noble of you to squander yourself on their behalf, but I doubt that they appreciate it." His blue eyes were as cold as glacial ice.

Judy thought she might be sick.

He waited, his expression filled with grim amusement. "What, no comment?"

"None." She threw the reins over Princess's head. "Thank you for the ride, John, I found it quite exhilarating." Her chin held at a proud angle, she mounted and silently rode away, her back rigid.

McFarland watched her go and viciously slammed his boot against the sand. He didn't know what had made him speak to her like that. He'd known from the moment he'd seen her picture that she was like no other woman he'd ever encountered. Another woman would have spit angry words back at him for the unprovoked attack. Judy hadn't. She'd revealed courage and grace, a rare combination. McFarland didn't know if he'd ever seen the two qualities exemplified so beautifully in any one woman. Most females were interested in his power and his wealth. No one had cared enough to call him by his first name.

He didn't like the feelings Judy Lovin aroused in him. Studying her picture was one thing, but being close to her, feeling the vital energy she exuded, watching her overcome her natural reserve had all greatly affected him.

Judy was good—too good for the likes of him. He chewed up little girls like her and spit them out. He didn't want to see that happen to Judy.

What an odd position to be in, he mused darkly. He had to protect her from himself.

Chapter Three

Princess's hind feet kicked up sand as Judy trotted the horse along the virgin beach. Her thoughts were in turmoil. What a strange, complex man John McFarland was. His eyes had been gentle and kind, almost laughing when he'd asked her to tell him about herself, and yet he'd obviously known everything there was to know about her. Her cheeks burned with hot humiliation that he'd discovered what a fool she'd made of herself over Richard. She'd been so trusting, so guileless with her affection and her heart . . . so agonizingly stupid to have fallen in love with a married man. The pain of Richard's deception no longer hurt Judy, but her own flagrant stupidity continued to cause excruciating embarrassment.

Judy was so caught up in her thoughts that she didn't notice the children at first. Their laughter filled the cool morning air and she gently drew in her reins, slowing the roan's gait. As always, the gentle mare's response was quick and sure to Judy's lightest touch.

"Princess, look," she said, her voice filled with excitement. "Children." They were playing a game of hide-and-seek, darting in and out of the jungle and rushing to the water's edge. Judy counted seven children, all between the ages of eight and twelve, from what she could guess.

They didn't appear to notice her, which was just as well since she didn't want to disturb their game. The smallest, a boy, was apparently chosen as "it" and the others scattered, smothering their laughter as they ran across the sand.

Judy lowered herself from the saddle.

Her action must have drawn their attention because the laughter stopped abruptly. She turned around to find all the youngsters running to hide. Only the one small boy remained.

Judy smiled. "Good morning," she said cautiously, not wanting to frighten him.

He remained silent, his deep brown eyes serious and intense.

Digging deep into the pocket of her jodhpurs, Judy pulled out two sugar cubes. The first she fed to Princess, placing it in the palm of her hand and holding it out to the mare, who eagerly nibbled it up. The second sugar cube she held out to the youth.

He eyed it for a long moment before finally stepping forward and grabbing it out of her hand. Quickly, he jumped away from her. Holding it in his own palm, he carefully approached the horse. When Princess lowered her sleek head and ate the cube from his hand, he looked up and grinned broadly at Judy.

"She's really very gentle," Judy said softly. "Would you like to sit in the saddle?"

He nodded enthusiastically and Judy helped him mount the tall mare.

Astride Princess, the boy placed both hands on the saddle horn and sat up straight, as though he were a king surveying his kingdom. Gradually, one at a time, the other children walked out from their hiding places in the edge of the lush jungle.

"Good morning," Judy greeted each one. "My name is Judy."

"Peter."

"Jimmy."

"Philippe."

"Elizabeth."

"Margaret."

They all rushed toward her, eager to be her friend and perhaps get the chance to ride her beautiful horse.

Judy threw up her hands and laughed. "One at a time, or I'll never be able to remember." She laid her hand on the slim shoulder of one of the younger girls. "I'm pleased to make your acquaintance." She was rewarded with a toothless smile.

From the ridge high above the beach, McFarland looked down on the scene below, a silent witness to Judy's considerable charm. She was a natural with children, and although he shouldn't be surprised at the way they gravitated toward her, he was. More times than he could count, he'd come upon the island children playing in the surf or along the beach. Usually he saw little more than a fleeting glimpse of one or two running away as though he were the devil incarnate. To them, he probably was.

Until he'd watched Judy weave her magic over these simple children, McFarland hadn't given a second thought to the few families who made this island their home. He allowed them to remain on St. Steven's, not for any humanitarian reasons, but simply because his feelings toward them were indifferent. They could stay or leave as they wished.

Unfortunately, he couldn't say the same thing about Judy Lovin. The sound of her laughter swirled like early morning mist around him. As he watched her now with these children, an unwilling smile touched the hard edges of his mouth. He, too, was a victim of the magic she wove so carelessly across his island.

He didn't like it, not one damn bit.

Sharply pulling back Midnight's reins, McFarland turned the horse and rode toward the other side of the island as if the fires of hell were licking at his heels.

By the time Judy returned to the house, McFarland had already eaten breakfast and sequestered himself in his offices. Judy wasn't disappointed. She'd purposely stayed away in an effort to avoid clashing with him a second time that morning. The man greatly puzzled her and she didn't know how to react to him.

Feeling increasingly unsettled as the morning turned to midday, she ordered a light lunch and ate in her room. In the afternoon, she swam in the Olympic-sized pool, forcing herself to swim lap after lap as she worked out her confusion and frustration. She had no clue as to why McFarland had sent for her other than to torment her family, and she hated to think that he would purposely do so. If she'd understood him better, she might be able to read his motive.

Breathless from the workout, Judy climbed out of the pool and reached for her towel, burying her face in the plush thickness. As she drew the material over her arms and legs, goose bumps pricked her skin and she realized that she was being watched. A chill shivered up her spine and she paused to glance around. She could see no one, but the feeling persisted and she hurriedly gathered her things.

In her own rooms, Judy paced, uncertain and unsettled. Deciding what she would do, she sat at the large desk and wrote a long, chatty letter to her father and brother. The hallway was silent when she came out of her room. She hesitated only a moment before making her way down the stairs and into the wing of the house from where she suspected McFarland ruled his empire.

"Miss Lovin?"

Avery Andersen's voice stopped her short when she turned a corner and happened upon a large foyer. "Hello," she said with feigned brightness. "I apologize if I'm intruding."

Avery stood, his hands pressing against the top of his desk as he leaned forward. "It's no intrusion," he said, obviously ill at ease at her unexpected appearance.

Judy hated to fluster the dear man. "I have some letters I'd like to mail."

"Of course."

Judy raised questioning eyes to his. "They're to my family?" She made the statement a question, asking if there would be any objection. "Is there regular mail delivery to the island?"

"All correspondence is handled by courier."

"Then there wouldn't be any objection to my writing my father?"

"None whatsoever."

Judy hated to be suspicious, but Avery didn't sound all that confident, and it would be so easy for him to deceive her.

"I'll see to it personally if that will reassure you, Miss Lovin." McFarland's voice behind her was brisk and businesslike.

Judy blushed painfully as she turned to face him. "I'd appreciate that," she said, stammering slightly. The potent virility of his smile caused her to catch her breath. That morning, when riding, he'd been sneering at her and now she could feel her pulse react to a simple twist of his mouth.

"Thank you, John," she said softly.

"John?" Avery Andersen echoed, perplexed, but his voice sounded as though it had come from another room—another world.

"Would you care to see my office?" McFarland asked, but the sparkle in his deep blue eyes made Judy wonder if he was silently taunting her. She felt the same way the fly must have when the spider issued a similar invitation.

"I don't want to interrupt your day." Already she was retreating from him, taking small, even steps as she backed away from Avery Andersen's desk. "Perhaps another time."

"As you wish." His eyes gentled perceptively at

49

her bemused look. "We'll talk tonight at dinner."

The words were as much a command as an invitation. Without question it was understood that she would be in the dining room when called.

Judy nodded. "At dinner."

By the time she closed the doors to her suite, her heart was thumping wildly. She attempted to tell herself she feared John McFarland, but that wasn't entirely true—the man was an enigma. Instead of gauging her responses by his mood, Judy decided she could only be herself.

She dressed for dinner in a skirt and blouse that had been favorites of her father's. Charles had claimed that the lovely pink and maroon stripes enhanced the brown of her eyes, reminding him of her mother.

At the top of the stairs, Judy placed her hand on the railing and paused. She was eager for this dinner, yet apprehensive. Her stomach turned over at the thought of food, but she yearned to know the man, "the Beast." Why he'd brought her to St. Steven's had yet to be answered. She had a right to know; she needed to know. Surely it wasn't too much to ask.

He was standing by the fireplace, sipping wine, when she entered the dining room. Once again she was struck by his virility. He, too, had dressed formally, in a pin-striped suit that revealed broad, muscular shoulders and narrow hips.

"Good evening, Judy."

She smiled and noted that he'd used her given name

for the first time. A little of the tension drained out of her.

"John."

"Would you care for a glass of white wine before dinner?"

"Please." The inside of her mouth felt as though a field of cotton had taken root. The wine would help or it could possibly drown her sadly lacking wit. As he approached her with a full goblet, Judy was unsure if she should take it. His burning blue eyes had the power to sear her soul and they burned into her now. Without realizing what she was doing, Judy reached for the wine, gripping the slim base of the glass as though it were a life ring in a storm-tossed sea.

"Why do you hate my father?" she asked, the demanding words slipping from her mouth without warning as she met his bold gaze.

"On the contrary, I hold him in high regard."

Judy's eyes widened with disbelief.

"Charles Lovin has more grit than twenty men half his age."

"You mean because he's managed to hold you off against impossible odds?"

"Not so impossible," McFarland countered, before taking a sip of wine. "I did allow him a means of escape."

Judy digested his statement, baffled by his reasoning. "You wanted me on the island," she said softly.

"Yes, you."

It wasn't as though he coveted her company. In the

two long days since her arrival, he'd barely spoken to her, indeed he seemed to avoid doing so.

"But why? What possible good am I to you?"

"None at all. I require no one." A hardness descended over his features then, and his eyes narrowed, steely and withdrawn, effectively shutting her out. His face revealed his arrogance and an overwhelming pride. A troubled frown creased Judy's brow. Pain filled her breast and she yearned with every womanly part of her to ease the hurt from his life. She longed to understand what made him the way he was. Somehow, somewhere, someone cruel and heartless had mortally wounded John McFarland's tender spirit. From the torment revealed in his eyes, she knew the scars hadn't healed.

"Am I to be your slave?" she asked, without anger, her voice smooth and even.

"No."

"Y-your pet?"

"Don't be ridiculous," he shouted. "You're free to do as you wish."

"Can I leave?"

He gave a curt laugh then and took a sip of his wine. "You are here to amuse me."

"For how long?"

He shrugged. "Until you no longer do so."

Muted footsteps distracted Judy's attention to the manservant who stood just inside the dining room. He nodded once in McFarland's direction.

"I believe our dinner is ready. Chicken Béarnaise."

He moved to her end of the table and held out her chair for her. Judy was grateful for the opportunity to sit down. Her legs felt as wobbly as cooked spaghetti. No man had ever affected her the way John did. He claimed he needed no one, and by all outward appearances he was right.

Once she was seated, John claimed the chair at the opposite end of the long table.

Without ceremony, Judy spread the soft linen napkin in her lap. "I happened upon some children today," she said conversationally after several tense moments.

"There are a number of families who live on the island."

"They're quite friendly. At first I wasn't sure they spoke English, but I soon realized that they speak it so fast that it sounds like a foreign language."

John smiled at that. "I haven't had the opportunity to talk to them myself, but I'll keep that in mind when I do."

"They asked about you."

"The children?"

"Yes, they call you the Dark Prince."

A brief smile flickered over his face. "The natives prefer to hide from me."

"I know."

Good humor flashed in his eyes as he studied her. Once again, she'd surprised him. He'd expected her to be outraged, spitting angry tirades at him, ruining his meal. Instead, she sat at the end of his table with the subtle grace of royalty when he knew she must be dying on the inside at his callousness.

"Since they call me the Dark Prince, did they give you a name?"

Judy hesitated and shifted her gaze. "I asked them to call me Judy."

"But they didn't."

"No." A dark color invaded her already flushed face. Swallowing became difficult.

"Tell me what they decided to call you."

"I—I'd prefer not to."

"Finding out would be a simple matter," he said in low, non-threatening tones.

Judy found little amusement in her predicament. "They called me 'the Dark Prince's woman.' I tried to explain that I was only a friend, but it didn't seem to do any good. I know this probably embarrasses you, but I couldn't seem to change their minds."

The laughter drained from McFarland's eyes. He'd meant to tease her, mock her innocence, but she was concerned that these people, these nonentities who occupied his land, had offended him by suggesting she was his woman. He felt as though someone had delivered him a swift kick in the behind. He raised his eyes to her, studying her to be certain she wasn't taunting him, and knew in his heart it wasn't in her to insult man or beast. And he was both.

Their meal arrived and McFarland realized he had little appetite. "Do you like the island?" he asked, wanting to hear her speak again. The sound of her voice was soothing to him.

"It's lovely."

"If there's anything you wish, you need only ask."

"There's nothing." Judy felt unsure. His tone, his look, everything about him had changed. His mocking arrogance had vanished, evaporated into the heavy night air. No longer did he look as though he meant to admonish her for some imagined wrong, or punish her for being her father's daughter. She found it impossible to eat.

"Do you dislike the solitude?"

She searched his face, wondering why he cared. "It's not Manhattan, but I don't mind. To be honest, I needed a vacation and this is as close to paradise as I'm likely to find."

"You've napped."

She nodded, chagrined.

"You're to have complete run of the house and island."

"Thank you, John," she said humbly, "you've been very kind."

Kind? He'd been kind to trap her into staying on the island? Kind to have blackmailed her into leaving everything familiar in her life? He stared at her, not understanding how she could even suggest such a thing. Abruptly, he pushed his plate aside and stood. "If you'll excuse me, I have some business matters that require my attention."

"Of course."

He stormed out of the room then, as though she had greatly offended him. For a full minute, Judy sat frozen, uncertain of what had transpired between them. He had seemed to want her company, then despised it.

She, too, had no desire to finish her meal, and feeling at odds with herself, she stood. The evening was young and she had no intention of returning to her rooms. John had claimed that she could freely explore the house and she had yet to see half of it.

Judy never made it beyond the center hall. The doors were what had attracted her most. The huge mahogany panels stretched from the ceiling to the polished floor, reminding her of ancient castles. Unable to resist, she twisted both handles, pushed open the massive doors and entered the dimly lit room.

She paused just inside, and a sigh of pure pleasure slipped from her throat. A library, elegantly decorated with a handful of comfortable leather chairs, two desks and a variety of tables and lamps. Every available wall was filled with books. If she'd inadvertently stumbled upon a treasure, Judy couldn't have been more pleased. A turn of the switch bathed the room in light and she hurried forward to investigate.

An hour later, when the clock chimed, Judy was astonished to realize that she'd been longer than a few minutes. Reverently, she folded back the pages of a first edition of Charles Dickens's *A Christmas Carol.* Each book produced a feeling a respect and awe. Mingled with the classics were volumes of modern literature; one entire wall was dedicated to nonfiction.

With such a wide variety to choose from, Judy finally selected a science fiction novel by Isaac Asimov. She sat in the high-backed leather chair and read for an hour before slipping off her shoes and curling her feet beneath her. Suddenly thirsty, she went to the meticulous stainless-steel kitchen and made herself a cup of tea. Carrying it into the library, Judy returned to her chair.

McFarland found her there after midnight, sleeping contentedly in the chair, her legs curled beneath her. Her head was nestled against the upholstery with one arm carelessly tossed over her face. The other arm dangled limply at her side so that the tips of her fingers barely touched the Persian carpet. Transfixed, he stood there for a long moment studying her, unable to look away.

A tender feeling weakened him, and he sat in the chair opposite hers. For a long time, he was content to do nothing but watch her sleep. He wondered at the wealth of emotion she aroused in him. He knew it wasn't love; it wasn't even close. He felt protective toward her, and yearned to take away the troubles that plagued this young woman's life. Surprisingly, he wanted her to be happy.

She looked as innocent as a child, but was very much a woman. She was gentle and kind, angelic without being saintly. Honorable without being lofty. Generous without being benign. He'd never known a woman like her, and was suddenly shocked to find himself consumed with fear. He could hurt

Judy Lovin, hurt her beyond anything she'd known in her life, hurt her more than Richard, who had stolen her trust and wounded her heart with his greed.

McFarland knew she would fall in love with him at the slightest encouragement. His conjecture wasn't based on ego, but on the knowledge that Judy, by nature, was giving and loving. If he were to ask, she would deny him nothing. His power over her frightened him, but that wasn't what stopped him from using her love. He wasn't any knight in shining armor. No, the simple truth was that Judy's control of him was more terrifying than any pleasure he would obtain in gaining her heart.

He thought about waking her and it seemed only natural to lean over and kiss her. Her lips would be soft and nimble under his. In his mind, he pictured her raising her arms and hugging his neck. She would smile at him and they'd stare at each other, uncertain of what to say. She'd blush in that special way she had that made her all the more beautiful, and her thick lashes would fan her cheek as she struggled to hide her feelings from him.

Forcefully, McFarland's fingers clenched the arm of the leather chair. He'd have a maid wake her and see her to her room. At this rate, he'd end up spending the night with her if he didn't leave.

She was just a woman, he reminded himself, and no doubt there were like a million others just like her. Who needed her? Not John McFarland.

"Midnight," Judy urged, standing on the bottom rung of the corral fence. "If you want it, you'll have to come to me." She held out the carrot to the prancing black stallion who snorted at her and pawed the ground.

"It's yours for the taking," she said soothingly. Winning the trust of the sleek, black horse had become paramount in the four days that had passed since the night she'd fallen asleep in the library. John had purposely been avoiding her; Judy was convinced of that. The only times they were together were at dinner, and he was always preoccupied with business, avoiding conversation and generally ignoring her.

Judy wasn't offended as much as bemused. At any moment, she half expected to receive word that he no longer required her presence on St. Steven's, or some other stiffly worded decree. She wouldn't mind leaving, although she would miss the children who had fast become her friends. She'd been on the island a week now and surely that was enough time to serve whatever purpose he warranted.

But she would miss the children. She met them daily now on the beach. They brought her small, home-made gifts; a flower pot and a hat woven from palm leaves, both cleverly done. A huge conch shell and a hundred smaller ones had been given to her with great ceremony. In return she told them stories, laughed at their antics and played their games. She met their mothers and visited their homes. She would miss them, but she wouldn't forget them.

"Midnight," she coaxed anew. "I know you want this carrot." If John wouldn't allow her to be his friend, then she'd work on the horse. Judy found several comparisons between the two; both were angry, arrogant and devilishly proud.

The horse remained in the farthest corner of the corral, determined to ignore her, just as John seemed determined to ignore her existence.

"I suppose all the women tell you how good-looking you are?" she said with a soft laugh. "But I'm not going to say that. As it is, you're much too conceited."

Midnight bowed his powerful head and snorted angrily.

"I thought that would get you." Jumping down from the fence, Judy approached the gate. "You're really going to make me come to you, aren't you?"

The stallion pranced around the yard, his tail arched and proud.

"You devil," Judy said, with a loud sigh. "All this time together and you're more stubborn now than when I started."

The horse continued to ignore her.

"What if I told you I had a handful of sugar cubes in my pocket?" She patted her hip. "Sweet, sweet sugar cubes that will melt in your mouth." As she spoke, she released the clasp to the gate and let herself inside the corral.

Midnight paused and stared at her, throwing his

head to and fro. "You'll have to come to me, though," she said softly.

His hoof dug at the hard dirt.

"Honestly, horse, you're more stubborn than your master."

She took three steps toward the huge black stallion, who paused to study her. He jerked his neck, tossing his thick black mane into the air.

With one hand on her hip, Judy shook her head. "You don't fool me one bit."

Someone approached from behind her, but Judy ignored the sound of footsteps, suspecting Sam. He was bound to be angry with her. He'd told her repeatedly not to get inside the corral, but since Midnight refused to come to her, she had no choice.

"Don't move." John's steel-edged words cut through her. "If you value your life, don't move."

Chapter Four

Judy went still, her heart pounding wildly. She wanted to turn and assure John that Midnight wouldn't hurt her. She longed to tell him that she'd been working for days, gaining the stallion's trust. All her life she'd had a way with animals and children. Her father claimed she could make a wounded bear her friend. Midnight had a fiery nature; it was what made him such a magnificent horse. He'd been a challenge, but he would never purposely injure her. But Judy said none of these things. She couldn't.

John's voice had been so cold, so cutting, that she dared not defy him.

The clicking sound behind her told Judy that Midnight's master had entered the corral. He walked past her and his clipped, even stride revealed his fierce anger. He didn't spare her a glance and from the hard, pinched look around his eyes, she was glad.

Midnight pranced around the corral, his eyes on the two invaders in his private world. His satiny black head was held high and proud, his tail arched, his feet kicking up loose dirt.

McFarland gave one shrill whistle to which the stallion responded without delay. Midnight cocked his head and galloped past Judy to his master's side, coming to an abrupt halt. He kicked the dirt once and lowered his head. With one smooth movement, McFarland gripped the horse's mane and swung his weight onto the stallion's back. Midnight violently protested against the unexpected action and reared, kicking his powerful front legs.

Judy sucked in her breath, afraid that McFarland hadn't time to gain control of the animal. She was wrong; when the horse planted his feet on the ground, John was in charge.

"Get out."

The words were sharp enough to slice through metal. He didn't so much as look at her, but then he didn't need to for her to feel his contempt and anger. Judy did as he requested.

McFarland circled the paddock a few times before

swinging off the stallion's back and joining her at the corral gate.

"You stupid idiot," he hissed. He grabbed her by the shoulders and gave her one vicious jerk. "You could have been killed."

When he released her, Judy stumbled backward. Her eyes were wide with fear. No one in all her life had ever spoken to her in such a menacing tone. No one had dared to raise a hand to her. Now she faced the wounded bear, and was forced to admit that Charles Lovin had been wrong; John McFarland was a beast no woman could tame.

"Who the hell let you inside the corral?"

Her throat had thickened, making speech impossible. Even if she had been able to answer him, she wouldn't have. Sam had no idea she'd ever been near Midnight.

"Sam!" McFarland barked the stable man's name with marked impatience.

The older man rushed out of the barn, limping. His face was red and a sheen of perspiration broke out over his forehead.

McFarland attacked him with a barrage of swear words. He ended by ordering the man to pack his bags.

Sam went pale.

"No," Judy cried.

McFarland turned on her then, his eyes as cutting as his words. He stood no more than a foot from her, his whole being bearing down on her as he shouted, using language that made her pale. Her eyes widened as she searched his face, attempting to hide her fear. She squared her shoulders with some difficulty. Her chin trembled with the effort to maintain her composure as she squarely met his cold gaze, unwilling for him to know how much he intimidated her.

McFarland couldn't make himself stop shouting at her. The boiling anger erupted like a volcano spitting fire. By chance, he'd happened to look out his window and seen Judy as she opened the corral gate. The fear had nearly paralyzed him. All he could think of was getting to her, warning her. A picture of Midnight's powerful legs striking out at her had driven him insane. He hadn't been angry then, but now he burned with it.

From her pale features, McFarland could see the shock running through Judy's veins as the pulse at the base of her throat pounded frantically. Still, the words came and he hated himself for subjecting her to his uncontrollable tantrum.

"Anyone who pulls an asinine trick like this doesn't deserve to be around good horseflesh," he shouted. "You're a hazard to everyone here. I don't want you near my stables again. Is that understood?"

Her head jerked back as though he'd slapped her. Glistening tears filled her eyes.

"Yes." She nodded weakly, signaling that she would abide by his edict.

She left him then, with such dignity that it took all his strength not to run after her and beg her forgiveness.

The air was electrified and McFarland rammed his hand through his thick hair. Sam stood there, accusing him, silently reprimanding him with every breath. The older man had once been a friend; now his censure scorched McFarland.

"I'll be out of here by morning," Sam muttered, and with a look of disgust, he turned away.

The remainder of the day was a waste. McFarland couldn't stop thinking of what he'd said to Judy and experienced more than a twinge of conscience. Lord, that woman had eyes that could tear apart a man's soul. When he'd ordered her to stay away from the horses, she'd returned his look with confused pain, as though that was the last thing she'd expected. He had wanted to pull her into his arms, hold her against his chest and feel the assurance of her heart beating close to his. Instead, he'd lashed out at her, attacked her with words, unmercifully striking at her pride when all he'd really wanted to do was protect her.

His vehement feelings shocked him most. He tried to tell himself that Judy deserved every word he'd said. She must have been crazy to get into a pen with an animal as unpredictable as Midnight. He'd warned her about him; so had Sam. Anyone with a brain in his head would have known better. There were times when even he couldn't handle that stallion.

Damn! McFarland slammed his fist against the desktop. He couldn't afford to feel like this toward a woman. Any woman, and most particularly Judy Lovin.

• • •

As she came down the stairs for dinner that evening, Judy's stomach tightened and fluttered with raw nerves. Her face continued to burn with humiliation. She would have much preferred to have dinner sent to her room and completely avoid John, but she had to face the beast for Sam's sake.

"Good evening, John," she said softly, as she entered the dining room.

He stood with his back to her, staring out the window. He turned abruptly, his eyes unable to disguise the surprise. From all appearances, he hadn't expected to see her.

"Judy."

They stood staring at each other before taking their places at the elegant table.

Not a word was exchanged during the entire meal. In all her memory, Judy couldn't recall a more awkward dinner. Neither had much appetite; eating was a pretense. Only after their plates had been removed and their coffee poured did she dare to appeal to the man across the table from her.

"Although I would prefer never to speak of what happened this afternoon, I feel I must talk to you about Sam."

John took a sip of his coffee. His eyes narrowed slightly, affronted that she would approach him on a matter he was sure to consider none of her business.

She clenched her napkin and forced herself to continue. "If you make Sam leave the island you might as well cut off both his legs. St. Steven's is his home; the horses are his family. What happened wasn't his fault. He'd told me repeatedly to stay away from Midnight. If he'd known I'd gone into that corral he would have had my hide. I snuck in there when Sam wasn't looking. He doesn't deserve to lose everything because of me."

John lowered his cup to the saucer without speaking.

"You may be a lot of things, John McFarland, but I trust you to be fair."

He arched his brows at that comment. This woman had played havoc with his afternoon, caused him to alienate a man he'd once considered a friend, and now she seemed to believe that by pleading softly she could wrap him around her little finger.

"Sam leaves in the morning, as scheduled."

Without ceremony, she rose from her chair. Her eyes held his, round with disbelief. "I see now that I misread you. My judgment is usually better, but that isn't important now." With nothing more to say, she turned to leave the room. After only a few steps, she paused and looked back. "My father once told me something, but I didn't fully appreciate his wisdom until this moment. He's right. No man is so weak as one who cannot admit he's wrong."

By the time she reached her rooms, Judy discovered she was shaking. She sat on the edge of her mattress and closed her eyes. The disillusionment was almost more than she could bear. She'd been wrong, very wrong about John McFarland. He was a wild, untamable beast—the most dangerous kind of animal . . . one without a heart.

Several hours passed, and although John had forbidden her to go near the stables again, Judy couldn't stay away. She had to talk to Sam, tell him how deeply sorry she was.

She changed from her dress into shorts and a light T-shirt. As usual the house was silent as she slipped down the stairs and out the front door.

Even the night seemed sullen and disenchanted. The air was still and heavy, oppressive. The area around the house was well lit, but the stable was far enough away to be enveloped in heavy shadows. The moon shone dimly.

As Judy walked along the path that led to the stables, she felt a chill invade her limbs. She longed for home and the comfort of familiarity. Folding her arms around her middle, she sighed. She tried not to think about how long John intended to keep her on the island. Surely he would send her away soon. After the incident with Midnight, he would be eager to be rid of her. She was a thorn in his side—a festering one.

Not for the first time did she feel like an unwelcome stranger to the island. Although she'd done everything possible to make the best of the situation, she was still John's prisoner. In the days since her arrival, she'd struggled to create some normalcy in her life. She had begun to feel at ease. Now that had changed.

Without access to Princess, she wouldn't be able to see the children as frequently and with Sam's dismissal, the servants would avoid her, fearing they, too, would lose their positions. Loneliness would soon overwhelm her.

The door to the stable was open, revealing the silhouette of Sam's elongated shadow. His actions were quick and sure and Judy strained her ears, thinking she heard the soft trill of his whistle.

"Evening, Sam," she said, pausing just inside the open doorway."

"Miss Lovin." His eyes brightened with delight, then quickly faded as he glanced around. "Miss Lovin, you shouldn't be here . . ."

"I know," she said gently, interrupting him. "I came to tell you how sorry I am."

He shrugged his thick shoulders, seemingly unconcerned. "Don't you bear that any mind. It's all taken care of now."

The words took a moment to sink into Judy's bemused mind. "You mean you aren't leaving?"

Sam rubbed the side of his jaw and cocked his head. "I've never known Mr. McFarland to change his mind. A man doesn't become as wealthy as that one without being decisive. I knew I'd done wrong to let you get close to that stallion—I figured I deserved what I got. Can't say that I agree with the way he flayed into you, though, you being a lady and all, but you took it well."

"You aren't leaving the island?" Judy repeated, still

not convinced she could believe what she was hearing.

"No. Mr. McFarland came to me, claimed he was wrong and that he'd overreacted. He asked me personally to stay on. I don't mind telling you I was surprised."

If Sam was surprised, Judy was astonished. She felt warm and wonderful. The sensation was so strong that she briefly closed her eyes. She hadn't misjudged John. He was everything she believed and a thousand times more.

"Mr. McFarland's here now," Sam continued, his voice low. "Midnight's still in the corral and he went out there. I don't suppose you saw him or you wouldn't be here." The man who ruled the stables removed his hat and wiped his forehead with the back of his hand, then he gave Judy a sheepish grin. "He didn't say anything to me about letting you in the stables again."

"I'll leave," she said, unable to hold back a smile. Sam was back in John's good graces, and she had become a threat.

The older man paused and looked around him before whispering, "You come see me anytime you want. Princess will miss you if you don't bring her a carrot every now and again."

Judy laughed and gently laid her hand upon his forearm. "Thank you, Sam."

His grin was off center, but she was grateful that she could count him as her friend.

Judy left the barn, intent on escaping before John discovered her presence. Her world had righted itself and there was no reason to topple it again so soon.

She was halfway to the house when she changed her mind, realizing how much she wanted to thank John. Like his stallion, John was dangerous and unpredictable. He was different from any man she'd ever known, and it frightened her how much she wanted to be with him. How much she wanted to thank him for not firing Sam.

John's shadow moved in and out of the dim moonlight as she approached. As Sam had claimed, he stood by the corral, one booted foot braced against the bottom rung, his arms looped over the top. The red tip of his cigarette glowed in the night, which surprised Judy since she'd never seen him smoke.

A moment later she joined him. "It's a lovely night, isn't it?" she said, tentatively leaning against the fence, searching for something to say.

McFarland tensed, his face hard and unyielding. He avoided looking at her. "There's a storm brewing."

"No," she countered with a soft smile. "The storm has passed."

He gave a low, self-mocking laugh. "I asked you to stay away from here."

"I won't come again if you wish."

What he did wish would have shocked her all the way to those dainty feet of hers, just as it had shocked him. He liked his women spicy and hot; Judy Lovin was sweet and warm.

"I'd like to show you something," she said, breaking into his thoughts. "But I need your trust."

He didn't answer her one way or the other. All evening he'd been toying with the idea of sending her back to her family and he was at a loss to understand why the idea no longer appealed to him. The woman had become a damn nuisance. She forced him to look deep within himself; she plagued his dreams and haunted his days. He hadn't had a moment's peace since she'd stepped onto the island.

"John, will you trust me for one moment?"

He tossed the half-smoked cigarette on the ground and smashed it with his boot. A muscle locked in his jaw and he turned his head slightly.

Standing on the bottom rung of the corral, she gave a shrill whistle that was an imitation of the one John had used earlier that day to attract Midnight's attention.

The stallion snorted once, jerked his head and casually walked over to her.

"Here, boy," she said, patting his nose and rubbing her hands and face over his as he nuzzled her with the affection of a lifelong friend. "No, I don't have any sugar cubes with me now, but I will another day. I wanted to show your master that we're friends."

Midnight gave a soft whinny and seemed to object when she stepped down and moved away.

McFarland wouldn't have been any more shocked if she'd pulled out a six-shooter and fired on him. She'd made Midnight look as tame as a child's pony. His throat tightened.

"I was never in any real danger," she explained in a low, gentle voice. "Midnight and I are friends. Most of his stubborn arrogance is show. It's expected of him and he likes to live up to his reputation."

"When?" McFarland growled.

"I've been working with him in the afternoons. We made our peace two days ago. He would even let me ride him if I wished, but he's your horse and I wouldn't infringe."

Why the hell not? She had infringed on everything else in his life! His peace of mind had been shot from the minute she'd turned those incredible eyes on him. She'd accused him of weakness in a voice as soft as an angel's, and condemned him with the noble tilt of her chin. She'd faced his angry tirade with a grace that had wounded his heart.

Without a word, he left her standing at the corral, not trusting himself to speak.

Hours later, unable to sleep, McFarland looked around his still bedroom. He didn't know what to make of Judy Lovin; she could be either demon or angel. She tamed wild animals, was beloved by children and caused his cynical heart to pound with desires that were only a little short of pure lust.

The maid woke Judy early the next morning just as dawn dappled the countryside.

"Mr. McFarland is waiting for you, miss."

Judy sat up in bed and rubbed the sleep from her eyes. "Mr. McFarland?"

"He's at the stables, miss."

"He wants me to go riding with him?"

"I believe so, miss."

With a surge of energy, Judy tossed back the covers and climbed out of bed. "Could you please tell him I'll be there in ten minutes?"

"Right away, miss."

Judy was breathless by the time she arrived at the stables. Princess was saddled and waiting for her; Midnight stood at the roan's side. John appeared from inside the barn.

"Good morning," she said brightly. He was dressed in black again, his eyes a deep indigo blue. "It's a glorious morning, isn't it?"

"Glorious," he echoed mockingly.

She decided to ignore his derision. The earth smelled fresh in the aftermath of the night's storm. The dew-drops beaded like sparkling emeralds on the lush foliage.

"Are you ready?" McFarland asked as he mounted.

"Any time." She swung her weight onto Princess's back.

As he had the first time she'd ridden with him, John rode like the very devil. Judy was able to keep pace with him, but by the time they reached the far side of the island, she was exhausted from the workout.

He slowed their pace and they trotted side by side on the flawless beach.

"You never cease to amaze me," he said, studying her. He'd ridden hard and long, half expecting her to fall behind, almost wishing she had.

"Me? I find you astonishing. Do you always ride like that?"

"No," he admitted sheepishly.

"You must have been born in the saddle."

"Hardly. I'd made my first million before I ever owned a horse."

"When was that?"

A slow, sensual smile formed as he glanced in her direction. "You're full of questions today, aren't you?"

"Does it bother you?"

He stared at her, bemused. "No, I suppose not."

"I imagine you had a colorful youth."

He laughed outright at that. "I'd been arrested twice before I was thirteen."

"Arrested?" Her eyes rounded.

"I thought that would shock you."

"But why?"

"I was a thief." He threw back his head and laughed. "Some say I still am."

Judy dismissed his joking with a hard shake of her head. "I don't believe that. You're an honorable man. You wouldn't take anything that didn't belong to you without a reason."

Her automatic defense of him produced a curious ache deep in his chest. There had been a reason—a damn good one. Someone had tried to cheat him. In like circumstances, he would respond identically. He wasn't bad, but in all his life, only one man had ever believed in him. From grade school, he'd been branded a renegade, a hellion. He'd been all that and more. He wouldn't be where he was today if he hadn't been willing to gamble. He had had to be tough, and God knew he was.

When he didn't respond, Judy sought his gaze. The look in his eyes made her ache inside. He wore the wounds of his past like medals of valor, but the scars were etched deep in his heart.

"What about you?" he taunted. "Haven't you ever done anything wrong?"

"You mean other than falling in love with a married man?"

The pain was so clear in her eyes that McFarland was ashamed to have asked the question.

"Actually, I have," she returned, recovering quickly. "I may not have been arrested but I could have been."

He arched both brows.

"Actually, I'm a thief, too, but I was smart enough not to get caught." She laughed outright, slapped the reins against Princess's neck and sped off, leaving a cloud of sand in her wake.

McFarland caught up with her easily.

She turned and smiled at him, her brown eyes sparkling. Dismounting, she brushed the wind-tossed hair from her face and stared into the sun. "I love this island. I love the seclusion and the peacefulness. No wonder you had to have it."

McFarland joined her on the beach. He knew he was going to kiss her, knew he'd regret it later, but he was past caring. He touched her shoulder and turned her so that she faced him, giving her ample opportunity to stop him if she wished.

Judy didn't. Her pulse surged as his mouth moved to cover hers.

His arms went around her, bringing her close as one hand moved up and down her spine, molding her to him. Her breasts grazed his chest and he groaned and dragged his mouth away. She tasted like paradise and now that he'd sampled her sweetness he didn't know how he could avoid wanting more. "I wish I hadn't done that," he said with a moan.

"I'm glad you did," she whispered.

"Dear God, don't tell me that."

"Yes . . ."

She wasn't allowed to finish as he cupped her face and kissed her again hungrily, unable to get enough of her. Sensuously, he rubbed his mouth back and forth over her moist lips until she groaned and leaned against him, letting him absorb her weight. He drew her so close their bodies were pressed full length against each other. He could feel the rise and fall of her softness against him as he lowered his hands and restlessly explored her back.

His fingers became tangled in her hair as he kissed her hard, his tongue greedily invading her mouth. He felt the tremor work its way through her at the unexpected intimacy and heard the soft sounds of passion that slid from her throat.

Instantly, he sobered, breaking off the kiss.

Judy sagged against him and released a long breath, pressing her forehead against his hard chest. "You kiss the same way you ride."

McFarland slowly rubbed his chin against the top of her head as a lazy smile touched the corners of his mouth. She made him tremble from the inside out. He'd been right the first time, he shouldn't have let this happen. He should have found the strength to resist. Now that he'd held her, now that he'd tasted her, there was no turning back.

"John?"

He wanted to blame her for what she did to him, punish her for dominating his thoughts and making him hunger for her touch, but his rage was directed solely at himself. It wasn't in him to lash out at her again, not for something she didn't deserve.

"I shouldn't have said those things."

"I know," she whispered, intuitively knowing he was talking about Midnight. "I understand."

"Why didn't you say something?"

"I couldn't—you were too angry. I'd frightened you."

He looped his arm around her shoulder. He should be begging for forgiveness, but all she seemed to do was offer excuses for him. "I want to make it up to you."

"There's no need. It's forgotten."

"No," he said forcefully. "I won't pass it off as lightly as that. Anything you want is yours. Just name it."

She went still.

"Except leaving the island." There must be a thousand things she longed to own, he thought. Jewels, land, maybe stocks and bonds. He would give them to her, he'd give her anything she asked for.

"John, please, there's no need. I . . ."

"Name it." His eyes hardened.

She bit the corner of her lower lip, realizing it would do little good to argue. He was making amends the only way he knew how—with money. "Anything?"

He nodded sharply.

"Then I want the school on the island remodeled. It's run down and badly in need of repairs and unsafe for the children."

Chapter Five

Paulo, a gleeful year-old baby, rested on Judy's hip as though he'd been permanently attached. Other children followed her around the cluster of homes as though she were royalty. The small party walked to the outskirts of the school yard, where the workers were busily constructing the new schoolhouse.

"Mr. McFarland told me the school will be ready by the end of the month," Judy told the children. The building had gone up so quickly that it had astonished Judy and the islanders. The day after she had made her request, a construction crew had arrived, followed quickly by several shiploads of building supplies.

Judy shuddered to think of the expense, but John hadn't so much as blinked when she said she wanted a school. And when John McFarland ordered something constructed, there were no delays.

Paulo's mother joined Judy and the other children. The baby gurgled excitedly, stretched out his arms and leaned toward his mother. Judy gave him a kiss and handed him over.

"Paulo likes you."

"As long as his mother isn't around," Judy responded with a soft laugh.

"The children are very happy," the shy mother added, looking toward the school.

"Don't thank me. Mr. McFarland is having it built, not me."

"But you're his woman and you're the one who told him of our need."

Judy had long since given up explaining that she wasn't John's "woman," although the thought wasn't as objectionable as when she'd first arrived. In the weeks since she'd first come to St. Steven's, her attitude toward John had altered dramatically. He was the beast her father claimed; Judy had seen that side of him on more than one occasion. But he possessed a gentleness, too, a loving-kindness, that had touched her heart.

Now that she knew him better, she hoped to understand his idiosyncrasies. He'd told her so little of his life, but from what she'd gleaned, he'd been abandoned at an early age and raised in a series of foster homes. A high-school teacher had befriended him, encouraged his talents and helped him start his first business. Although the teacher had died before John had achieved his financial empire, the island had been named after him—Steven Fischer.

Since the kiss they'd shared that early morning, Judy's relationship with John had altered subtly. As before, he didn't seek out her company and the only time that she could count on being with him was at dinner. She was allowed to take Princess whenever she wished, but the invitation to ride with John had come only twice. He treated her with the politeness due a house-guest, but avoided any physical contact, which told her that he regretted having kissed her.

Judy didn't regret it. She thought about that morning often, relived it again and again, fantasizing, wishing it hadn't ended so quickly.

Letters from her family arrived regularly now. Both her father and her brother worried about her, but Judy frequently assured them she was happy, and to her surprise, realized it was the truth. She missed her old life, her family and her home, but she kept them close in her heart and didn't dwell on the separation.

John had given no indication as to when she could return and she hadn't asked. For now she was content.

After spending the morning with the children, Judy returned to the house, wearing a wreath of flowers on her head like a crown. The children and Paulo's mother had woven it especially for her and she'd been touched by their generosity.

Since it was an hour until lunch, Judy decided to write her family and give John the letter at lunch. The library doors were open and beckoned her inside. Judy walked into the room.

McFarland sat at the desk, writing.

"John," she whispered, surprised. "I'm sorry, I didn't mean to intrude."

He glanced up and the heavy frown that creased his forehead relaxed at the sight of her. She wore a simple yellow sundress with a halo of flowers upon her thick, dark hair, and looked so much like a visitation of some heavenly being that he couldn't pull his eyes away from her.

"You didn't disturb me," he assured her.

"It's a fantastic morning," she said eagerly, seeking a topic to carry the conversation.

In the weeks since her arrival, Judy had acquired a rich, golden tan. Her healthy glow mesmerized him. "Beauty" did little to describe this woman, whose charm and winsome elegance had appealed so strongly to his heart. McFarland had never known anyone like her. Her gentle goodness wasn't a sugar coating that disguised a greedy heart. Judy Lovin was pure and good; her simple presence humbled him.

The memory of the one kiss they'd shared played havoc with his senses. He'd avoided touching her since, doing his utmost to appear the congenial host. The sweetest torment he'd ever endured was having her close and not making love to her. He feared what would happen if he kissed her again, and yet the dream of doing so plagued his sleep.

He had planned to return Judy to her family before now, but couldn't bring himself to do so. He was at odds with himself, realizing that it was inadvisable to continue to keep her on the island with him. If she'd revealed some signs of being unhappy and asked to return to New York, he would allow it, but Judy showed no desire to leave and he selfishly wished to keep her with him despite her family's constant pleading.

"I spent the morning with the children," Judy said, still only a few steps inside the room. "They're excited about the school."

John nodded, unconcerned. "Did they give you the flowers?"

She raised tentative fingers to her head, having forgotten about the orchid wreath. "Yes, the children are clever, aren't they?" Out of the corner of her eye, she caught sight of an elaborate chess set. When he didn't respond to her first question, she asked another. "Do you play?"

McFarland's gaze followed her own. "On occasion."

"Are you busy now?"

He glanced at his watch, more for show than anything. He was always busy, but not too busy to torture himself with her. "Not overly so."

"Shall we play a game, then?" She longed for his company. "That is, if it wouldn't be an intrusion."

His gaze held hers and it wasn't in him to refuse her anything. "All right," he agreed.

Her warm smiled rivaled the most glorious sunrise. "Good," she said, and brought the chess set to the desk and pulled up a chair to sit opposite him.

"Shall we make it interesting?" McFarland asked, leaning forward.

"Money?"

He grinned. "No."

"What then?"

"Let the winner decide."

"But . . ."

"How good are you?"

Judy dropped her gaze to the board. "Fair. If I lose, what would you want from me?"

Oh, Lord, what a question. The possibilities sent his blood pressure soaring. He wanted her heart and her soul, but not nearly half as much as he wanted to feel her sweet body beneath his own. The image clawed at his mind and nagged at his senses. He'd be her first lover; that alone was enough to force him to rein his desire.

"John?"

"What would I want?" he repeated hurriedly. "I don't know. Something simple. What about you; what would you want?"

Her bubbly laughter echoed off the book-lined walls in dulcet tones. "Something simple."

His eyes softened as he studied her. Afraid that he would be caught staring, McFarland tried to look away and discovered her eyes held his as effectively as a vise. A man would be tempted to sell his soul for her smile.

"It's your move."

McFarland forced his attention to the board, unaware that she'd placed her pawn into play. "Right." He responded automatically, sliding his own man forward.

By the sheer force of his will, he was able to concentrate on the game. Her technique was straightforward and uncomplicated and a few moves later, he determined that she revealed a weak strategy. He should be able to put her in checkmate within ten to fifteen minutes, but he wasn't sure he wanted to. If he were to lose, albeit deliberately, then he'd be obligated to give her "something simple." He thought about how she'd look in a diamond necklace and doubted that the jewels could compete with her smile. Emeralds would draw out the rich color of her deep brown eyes, but no necklace could do her eyes justice. A sapphire broach perhaps. No, not jewels. Furs . . .

"John? It's your turn."

Slightly embarrassed to be caught dreaming, he slipped his bishop forward with the intent of capturing her knight, which was in a vulnerable position.

Judy hesitated. "That wasn't a good move, John. Would you like to take it over?"

She was right, it wasn't a brilliant play, but adequate. "No, I released my hand from the bishop."

"You're sure?"

He studied the pieces again. He wasn't in any imminent danger of losing his king or the match. If he did forfeit the game it would be on his terms. "Even if this were a bad move, which it isn't," he added hastily, "I wouldn't change it."

Her eyes fairly danced with clever excitement. "So be it, then." She lifted her rook, raised her eyes to his before setting it beside his undefended king, and announced, "Checkmate."

Tight-lipped, John analyzed the play and was astonished to discover she was right. So much for her being straightforward and uncomplicated! The woman had duped him with as much skill as a double agent. The first couple of plays had been executed to give him a sense of false security while she set him up for the kill.

"I won," she reminded him. "And according to our agreement, I am entitled to something simple."

McFarland still hadn't taken his eyes off the chess board. The little schemer. Now that he'd seen how she'd done it, he was impressed with her cunning and skill. All right. He'd lost in a fair game; he was ready for her to name her price.

"Okay," he said a bit stiffly. "What would you like? A diamond necklace?"

She shook her head. "Oh, no, nothing like that."

"What then? A car?"

For an instant she was too stunned to reply. "Good heavens, no. It seems your idea of something simple and mine are entirely different."

"What do you want then?"

"Your time."

His expression grew puzzled. "My what?"

"Time," she repeated. "You work much too hard. I don't even recall an afternoon when you weren't cooped up in that stuffy office. You own a small piece of paradise; you should enjoy it much more often."

"So what's that got to do with anything?"

"For my prize I want us to pack a lunch and take it to the beach. It'll be a relaxing afternoon for us both."

He grinned at the idea that she would assume he had the time to do nothing but laze on the beach. Surely she wasn't so naive not to know he ruled a financial empire. Offices around the globe were awaiting his decisions. "I don't have time for that nonsense," he said finally with a crooked half smile. Sometimes he forgot how uncomplicated she was.

"That's a shame," Judy said, looping a dark strand of hair around her ear. "Unfortunately, you were the one who decided to place a wager on the match. You should never have made the suggestion if you weren't willing to follow through with it."

"I'll buy you something instead. I know just the thing."

Judy shook her head adamantly. "I would have sworn you were a man of your word. The only thing I want is this afternoon."

"Damn it, Judy," he shouted, and slapped his hand against the surface of the desk. "I can't afford to waste precious time lollygagging around the beach.

"Yes, John."

"There are cost sheets, reports, financial statements . . . that all must be reviewed this afternoon."

"Yes, John."

"Decisions to be made." His voice rose in volume with every word. "Offers to be considered."

Judy let neither his tone nor his words intimidate her. "I'll be at the door in one half hour and leave with or without you. But I honestly believe that you are a man of honor."

She left the room and McFarland continued to sit at the desk, hot with frustration. She had tricked him; she'd set him up, patiently waited and then waltzed in for the kill while he sat across from her like a lamb with its throat exposed. His laugh was filled with bitterness. Damn innocent woman. Tokyo Rose was more subtle than Judy Lovin!

At the appointed time, Judy stood in the foyer waiting for John. When he didn't come, she lingered for an additional five minutes. Deeply disappointed, she lifted the large wicker picnic basket and walked out of the house alone.

In his suite of offices, McFarland stood at the balcony door staring into space, thinking. It wasn't that he didn't have the time to spend lazing on the beach. If he truly wanted, he could have joined her. The problem was Judy. Every time he was with her, the need for her, his burning desire, dug deep talons into his chest. A curious ache tore at his heart. Perhaps his upbringing—or lack of one—was the problem. At no other time in his life had he wanted to know a woman the way he did Judy. He yearned to hold her in his arms and hear tales from her childhood, and tell her of his own. From the little bit she'd described, he'd recognized how close she'd been to her mother. She rarely spoke of her brother or father and McFarland didn't encourage it, fearing she missed them and would ask to be released.

For his own part, McFarland had told her more of his life than he'd ever revealed to anyone. Being with her made him weak in ways he couldn't explain. That kiss was a good example. He'd promised himself he wouldn't do it and then . . . His heart sneered at the simple memory of holding her in his arms and tasting her willing response. A low groan of frustration worked its way up the back of his throat and he momentarily closed his eyes.

Pivoting, he walked over to the liquor cabinet, poured himself a stiff drink and downed it in two swallows. He wanted her. This gut-wrenching soul-searching led to one thing and one thing only. He hungered to take Judy in his arms and kiss her sense-less until she knew a fraction of his desire. And when the moment came, she would smile up at him with those incredible eyes of hers and give him her very soul and ask nothing in return. His power was so frightening that he trembled.

"Mr. McFarland?" Avery Andersen stepped into the office.

"Yes," he snapped.

"I'm sorry to disturb you."

McFarland shook his head, dismissing the apology. "What is it?"

Avery shifted his feet and squared his shoulders. "It's Miss Lovin."

"Yes. Is there a problem? Is she hurt?" He strove to keep his voice unemotional, although his heart was hammering anxiously against his ribs.

"No . . . no. Nothing like that."

"Then what?" he asked, losing his patience. Avery ran a finger inside his stiff white collar.

"She's been on the island nearly a month now."

"I'm aware of that."

"I was wondering how much longer her family can expect to be kept waiting before she's returned."

"Have they been pestering you again?" Grim resolve tightened his features. Judy enjoyed the island; he could see no reason to rush her departure.

Avery gave one short, barely perceptible shake of his head and dropped his gaze. "No . . ."

"Then who's doing the asking?"

Avery squared his shoulders and slowly raised his gaze to his employer's. His lips parted and quivered slightly. "I am, sir."

"You?"

"That's right, Mr. McFarland."

"How long Miss Lovin stays or doesn't stay is none of your concern." His tone was cold and calculated.

"But, sir . . ."

"That'll be all, Avery."

He hesitated for a long moment before turning, white-lipped, and walking out of the room.

McFarland watched his assistant leave. Even his staff had been cast under her spell. Sam, who could be as mean as a saddle sore, rushed to do her bidding. Princess had never been groomed more frequently or better. When asked about the extra attention paid to the mare, Sam had actually blushed and claimed it was for Miss Lovin.

The maids fought to serve her. The chef somehow managed to learn her favorite dishes and cooked them to the exclusion of all else. Pleased by his efforts, Judy had personally gone to thank him and kissed the top of his shining bald head. The island children followed her like a pied piper. Even Midnight had succumbed to her considerable charm. McFarland wiped a hand over his face. The entire island rushed to fulfill her every command. Why the hell should he be exempt from yearning to please her?

"Avery," he barked.

"Sir." The other man rushed into the room.

"Cancel my afternoon commitments."

"Excuse me?" Incredulous disbelief widened the older man's eyes.

"I said wipe out any commitments I have for the remainder of the day."

Avery checked his watch. "Are you feeling ill, Mr. McFarland? Should I contact a doctor?"

"No. I'm going swimming."

Avery's eyes narrowed in disbelief. "Swimming?"

"In the ocean," McFarland explained, grinning.

"The one outside—the one here?"

"That's right." Purposefully, he closed the folder on his desktop lest he be tempted to stay. "Avery, when was the last afternoon you had free?"

"I'm not sure."

"Take this one off as well. That's an order."

An instantaneous smile lit up the fastidious man's face. "Right away, Mr. McFarland."

McFarland felt as young as springtime and as excited as a lover on Valentine Day as he walked through the house to his quarters and changed clothes. With a beach towel wrapped around his neck, he walked down the front lawn and searched the outskirts of the beach. He found Judy lying under the shadow of a tall palm tree. A large blanket was spread out in the grass and the picnic basket was opened. He glanced inside and there was enough food to hold off a siege.

Judy lay on her back with her eyes closed, soaking up the sun's golden rays. She appeared tranquil, but her thoughts were spinning. She shouldn't be on St. Steven's. She should be demanding to know when John intended to release her so she could return to her family. Instead she was lazing on the beach feeling sorry for herself because she'd misjudged John McFarland. Her pride was hurt that he would refuse such a simple request. She liked being with John; the highlight of her day was spending time with him. She savored those minutes, and was keenly disappointed when he chose to leave her. The kiss they'd shared had changed everything; nothing could be the same anymore. They had only come to trust each other enough to be friends; now they feared each other. The kiss hadn't satisfied their curiosity; it had left them yearning for more.

A soft protest sounded from her throat. She was falling in love with John. She didn't want to love him. He would hurt her and send her away when he tired of her. Nor did he want her love. It would embarrass him—and her—if he were ever to guess.

"You knew I'd come, didn't you?" McFarland said, standing above her.

Judy's eyes shot open, blinked at the bright sunlight and closed again. Shielding her eyes with her hand, she braced herself on one elbow and looked at him again. "John." She sat upright.

He didn't look pleased to be there, but she was too happy to care.

"Sit down." She patted the blanket beside her. "And no, I didn't know you were coming, but I'm happy that you did."

He snickered softly in disbelief and joined her. Looping an arm around his bent knee, he stared into the rolling blue surf. "I'll have you know I left McDonnell Douglas on the wire to fulfill this wager."

"They'll contact you tomorrow."

"You hope."

"I know," she said, hiding a smile. "Now don't be

93

angry with me. You were the one who suggested we make things interesting."

"Hell, why can't you be like every other woman in the world and request diamonds?"

"Because some things are worth more than jewels."

"What's the problem? Do you have so many that more don't interest you?" His face was hard and unyielding, but his anger was directed more at himself than Judy.

"My mother left me three or four lovely pieces." She slowly trailed her finger in the sand. "But I seldom wear jewelry." He wouldn't understand and it would be embarrassing to her if she were to explain that being with him was worth more to her than rubies and pearls.

A strained moment followed. "I shouldn't have snapped at you."

She turned to face him and was caught once again in his tortured gaze. Her breath froze in her lungs as her chest tightened. Not knowing what drove her, she raised her hand to his face, yearning to wipe away the hurt. John's eyes closed as her fingers lightly brushed his cheek. His beard nipped at her fingertips. He caught her hand, then, and raised his eyes to hers, kissing the sensitive inside of her hand.

The sensation of his tongue against her palm produced a soft gasp from Judy.

"I shouldn't do this," he said and groaned, directing her face to his. He kissed her cheek, her temple and her eyes.

They broke apart momentarily, and when he reached for her again, Judy met him halfway. This time the kiss was much deeper, and when he raised his head they were both dazed and more than a little shocked. The kiss was better, far better than either had anticipated.

McFarland rose to his knees, pulling Judy with him. Her look of innocent desire tore at his conscience. He hadn't meant to kiss her again; he feared hurting her more than he feared losing his wealth. But the soft, feminine feel of her as she brushed her breasts over his torso caused his blood to boil. And in the end, he kissed her again and again, slanting his mouth over hers until his heart thundered and roared. He lost himself in the unequaled taste of her. Her sweetness melted away years of loneliness. When she placed her trembling hand over his chest, it seared his flesh as thoroughly as a branding iron. At the moment, it wasn't in McFarland to protest.

John's kisses made Judy light-headed. The finest wine couldn't produce a sensation as potent as this. She trembled in his arms and when her gaze met his, her eyes were wide.

He dragged his gaze away from her, afraid of her angelic innocence.

"Let's swim."

Judy nodded and he helped her to her feet.

The turquoise water was only a few feet away and they stepped into the rolling surf together. The cool spray against her heated flesh took Judy's breath away.

John dove into an oncoming wave and Judy followed him. He broke the surface several feet from her, turned and waited for her to swim to him.

"Have you ever body surfed?" He shouted to be heard above the sound of the churning sea.

"No, but I'd like to."

"Good." He reached out and gripped her waist. "We'll take this wave together."

With no option, Judy closed her eyes and was thrust into the swelling wall of water. Her hold on John tightened as they were cast under the surface by a giant surge of unleashed power. The tide tossed them about as effortlessly as a grain of wheat caught in the wind.

Judy threw back her head and laughed once the wave passed them to wash up on the beach. "That was wonderful." She wrapped her arms around John's neck.

"You're slippery," McFarland said, using the excuse to draw her closer. His hand held her firmly against him, creating another kind of torture. His fingers brushed the wet strands of hair away from her face. Her pulse went wild at his gentle touch.

His eyes held hers and darkened just before his mouth crushed hers. Judy gave herself to the kiss, responding with all the love stored in her heart. The water took them again, but neither seemed concerned. When they broke the surface, Judy was breathless and weak.

McFarland's chest heaved. He had thought he

could escape his need for her in the water, but it hadn't worked that way. "You're even better in the water."

"Pardon?"

"Nothing," he grumbled.

She threw back her head and laughed. "You taste like salt water."

And she tasted like heaven. Good God, how was he ever going to let her go? "Judy?"

She wound her arms around his neck and smiled shyly. Maybe he would admit that he loved her. Her heart beat anxiously. It was a fanciful dream. Earning John's love would take more than a few playful moments in the surf. He had to learn to trust.

"Listen," he said in a low voice that sounded strangely like a groan. "I have to tell you something."

She lifted her head, fearing that the time had come for him to send her away.

"I'm leaving."

Her heart slammed against her breast. "When?"

"In the morning."

"How long?"

"A few days," he said, and continued to brush the wet hair from her face, although it had long since been smoothed into place. "Four, possibly five."

Perhaps he had decided to send her away. Her eyes must have revealed her distress.

"Will you wait for me here, Beauty?"

She nodded, overcome with relief.

"Good," he whispered, and greedily sought her mouth once again.

Not until he kissed her did she realize he hadn't called her Judy.

Chapter Six

John left just after dawn the next morning. Judy was awake and at the sound of muted voices from downstairs, she reached for her robe and rushed down the winding stairway. By the time she arrived, John had already left, but she could see his Jeep in the distance. She stood on the huge porch, leaning dejectedly against the thick marble column. She would have liked to have wished him well.

"Morning, Miss Lovin."

Judy straightened and turned toward Avery Andersen.

"Morning. I see John got off without a hitch."

"He should be away only a few days."

"Four at the most." She quoted what John had told her. Her gaze followed his disappearing figure until he was out of sight. "It won't be so bad."

"He's instructed me to see to your every wish."

She smiled. If she were to have a silly craving for pastrami from her favorite New York deli, Judy didn't doubt that speedy arrangements would be made.

"He doesn't go away often," Avery went on to explain as he straightened his bow tie. "He wouldn't now if it wasn't necessary."

Judy nodded. John hadn't wanted to leave her. She'd seen the regret in his eyes as they pleaded softly with her for understanding.

"Some claim McFarland's a recluse," Avery commented thoughtfully, studying Judy.

"No," she countered, and gently shook her head. "Not in the true sense of the word, but he cares a great deal for his privacy."

"He does at that," the older man agreed.

They turned to go back inside then, each walking through the wide doors and parting at the foot of the stairs.

Four days didn't seem long, Judy told herself as she dressed. The time would fly. She glanced at her watch; already fifteen minutes had gone.

Slumping onto the edge of the bed, Judy released a long, slow breath. She loved John and was only beginning to realize the full ramifications of blithely handing him her heart. Caring for him excited her, and made her afraid. John wouldn't be an easy man to love; he knew so little about it. Judy had been surrounded by it, smothered in it. Her love for John gave him an awesome power to hurt her and she wasn't convinced that telling him of her feelings would be in her best interests—or his.

The first day passed without incident. The second was equally dull. Mealtimes were the loneliest hours. She sat at the end of the table and experienced such an overwhelming sense of privation that she scolded herself for being so painfully dramatic.

Nothing seemed right without John. Not riding Princess around the island; not visiting the children; not letters to her family, not swimming.

She was lonely and bored, fidgety and at odds with herself. One man had toppled her world and a few days without him taxed the balance of her humdrum existence.

The night of the third day, Judy tossed and turned in her bed, unable to sleep. She missed John dreadfully and was angry with herself for feeling such a loss without him.

At midnight, she threw aside the blankets and silently crept down the stairs for a glass of milk, hoping that would help her insomnia. John's office was on the opposite side of the house from the kitchen, and Judy carried her milk with her to the opulently paneled suite, flipping on the lights. She silently slipped into his desk chair, tucking her bare feet under her, Briefly she closed her eyes, inhaling the scent of him. A smile curved her mouth. She could almost feel his presence and some of the ache eased from her heart.

Weary to the bone, McFarland entered the house and paused in the foyer, resisting the urge to climb the stairs and wake Judy. The thought of holding her sleepy head against his chest was almost more than he could bear.

The business meetings hadn't gone well and in part he blamed himself. Negotiations had come to an impasse and, in his impatience to return to the island, he had asked that the meeting be adjourned while both parties considered the lengthy proposals. He would have stayed in Dallas if he'd felt it would have done any good, but he figured it would be better to return to St. Steven's rather than buckle under to United Petroleum's unreasonable demands.

He paused, rubbed a hand over his face and smiled. He didn't need to wake Judy to feel her presence in his home. She was like the sweet breath of spring that brought the promise of summer. He had only to shut his eyes to see her bouncing down the stairs with a vitality that rivaled life itself. The sound of her laughter was like sparkling water bubbling over a short waterfall. Her smile could blot out the sun.

His heart constricted with emotion. He would surprise her first thing in the morning. Until then he would have to be content.

With that thought in mind, he headed toward his rooms, until a light in his office attracted his attention. It was unlike Avery to work this late unless there was a major problem. Frowning, McFarland decided he'd best check into the matter.

One step into his office and he stopped cold. Judy was curled up in the chair behind his desk, sound asleep. She was the picture of innocence with her head cocked to one side, the thick coffee-colored hair falling over her cheek. She wore a plain nightgown beneath an equally unfeminine robe. Neither did much to reveal the womanly curves beneath. However, McFarland had never experienced a stronger stab of desire. It cut through him, sharp and keen, and trapped the breath in his lungs.

Had it been any other woman, he would have kissed her until she was warm and willing in his arms, carried her into his room and satisfied his yearning with her lush body. He couldn't do that with Judy; her sweet innocence prevented that.

He hesitated, debating on how he should wake her. His impulse was to bend over and kiss her, but he feared that would never satisfy him and the potency of his desire would only shock her. Shaking her awake or calling her name might frighten her.

Of her own accord, Judy stirred and stretched her arms high above her head, arching her back and yawning loudly. She hadn't meant to fall asleep. When she opened her eyes, she discovered John standing on the other side of the desk from her. She blinked. At first she was convinced he wasn't real but the embodiment of her deepest desires. When she realized that he was indeed very much alive, she leaped from the chair, nearly tripping on the hem of her nightgown.

"John." She slapped her hand over her breast. "I'm so sorry . . . I don't know what came over me to come into your office. It must have shocked you to find me here. I . . . do apologize."

"My home is yours. No apology is necessary," he said softly as his gaze fell on the empty glass.

"I couldn't sleep." She brushed the array of hair

from her face, still flustered and more than a little embarrassed. "When did you get in?"

A smile twitched at the corners of his mouth. She looked like a guilty child who had been caught with her hand in the cookie jar. "Only a few minutes ago."

She clenched her hands together and smiled brightly, genuinely pleased that he had returned. "Welcome home."

"It's good to be here."

Judy tightened her hands to restrain the urge to run into his arms, hold onto him and beg him never to leave her again. Her heart continued to pound, but she didn't know if it was from being caught in his office or just the virile sight of him.

"Did anything happen while I was away?" he asked, reaching for his mail and idly flipping through it.

"Nothing important." She stood across from him, drinking in his presence as though he would disappear at any moment. "Are you hungry? I'd be happy to fix you something." She prayed he was famished, just so she would have an excuse to stay with him longer.

"Don't go to any trouble."

"I won't. Will a sandwich do?" She smiled then, inordinately pleased to be able to do this one small thing for him.

"A sandwich would be fine."

He followed her into the kitchen and pulled up a stool to a stainless-steel table while Judy opened the refrigerator and took out the necessary ingredients.

"How was the trip?" she asked, liberally slathering the bread with butter and mayonnaise before placing slices of turkey and tomato over it.

McFarland had never discussed his business matters with anyone outside of his office. The temptation to do so now was strong, but he didn't. "Everything went as expected," he said matter-of-factly, which was only half true.

Judy cut the sandwich into halves, set it on a plate and handed it to him. Then she poured them each a glass of milk and sat on a stool across from him.

Elbows braced against the tabletop, she cupped her face in her hands and studied him while he ate. Her brow creased with concern as she noted the lines of fatigue around his eyes and mouth. "You look exhausted."

"I am. I didn't make it to bed last night."

"The meetings didn't go well, did they?"

Her intuition surprised him; he hadn't thought he was that easy to read. "I didn't expect them to."

"What happened?"

McFarland shrugged. "I made an offer, they rejected it and came back with a counteroffer."

"And you rejected that?"

He paused, the glass halfway to his mouth. "Not exactly. Not yet, anyway," he elaborated.

"But you will?"

Again he shrugged, and his eyes met hers. "I'm not sure."

Judy continued to study John. He was physically exhausted, but the mental defeat weighed far heavier on him. As a young girl, she had often watched her mother soothe the tension from her father. Georgia Lovin hadn't offered suggestions; she had had no expertise in business, but she possessed the uncanny ability to get her husband to relax and talk out the problem so that he found the solution. Judy prayed that she could do the same for John.

"You want this deal, don't you?" she asked him softly.

McFarland nodded. "I've been working on it for over a year now. The offer I made United Petroleum is a fair one—hell, it was more than fair. But I'm at a disadvantage."

"Why?"

He set the glass down hard. "Because they damn well know I want this."

"I see."

"Now that you mention it, I may have appeared too anxious to settle." He couldn't deny his eagerness. He had wanted to get those papers signed so he could get back to the island and Judy, his mission accomplished. He'd thought he'd been more subtle, but perhaps not. "Let me explain," he said, taking a napkin and scribbling down a series of figures.

He spoke nonstop for fifteen minutes. Most everything he said was far beyond Judy's comprehension, although she pretended to understand every bit of it.

She nodded at the appropriate times and smiled when he finished.

"You're right," he said with a wide grin. "Damn, why didn't I think of that?"

Judy hadn't a clue as to what he was talking about, but it didn't seem to matter. The weariness was gone from his eyes. He stood and paced the kitchen.

"That's it," he said, and paused in front of her. "Has anyone ever told you what a marvel you are?" His hands cupped her face and he kissed her soundly.

Judy's breath lodged in her chest. "What was that for?" she asked in a voice that sounded strangely unlike her own.

"To thank you." He checked his watch. "It's late, but I think I'll contact my attorney and talk this latest strategy over with him."

"John," she protested. "It's one o'clock in the morning!"

"For the money I pay that man it shouldn't matter what time I call him."

Before she could protest further, John was at the kitchen door. He opened it, paused and turned back. "Will you ride with me in the morning?"

She smiled and nodded eagerly, grateful that he'd thought to ask.

In his office, McFarland emptied his briefcase and set the file for United Petroleum on his desktop. It struck him then, sharply. Without him knowing how, Judy had gotten him to reveal the minute details of this buy out. He'd told her everything without the least bit of hesitation. He didn't fear what she'd do with the information; there was nothing she could do.

What shocked him was that she had so completely gained his confidence that he cheerfully gave out industry secrets without a second thought. This woman tied knots a sailor couldn't untangle, and every one of them was strung around his heart, choking off his independence. She was quickly making herself essential.

He paused and rubbed his hand over his face as he analyzed the situation. McFarland didn't like the thought of a woman, any woman, controlling his life. Not one damn bit. Something had to be done to put an end to it.

At dawn Judy rushed to meet John at the stables. She had slept like a baby after leaving him. When the maid had come to wake her, she'd resisted climbing out of the warm bed, preferring to hold on to the memory of John's arms around her. It took her a moment to realize she'd been dreaming.

Midnight and Princess were saddled and waiting.

"Morning," she called to Sam and smiled at John, who immediately swung onto Midnight's back.

The burly trainer waved and Judy took a moment to stroke Princess's smooth neck before mounting. John's look remained stoic.

"How'd you sleep?" she asked when they'd gone only a couple of hundred feet. He was quiet, withdrawn and taciturn—nothing like the warm, gentle man he'd been when they'd parted.

"I didn't get to bed," he answered crisply.

"Oh, John, again? You must be ready to fall out of the saddle."

"No. After you left last night, I got to analyzing the proposal and decided there were still more things I wanted to change before I talked to Butterman."

Judy assumed Butterman was his attorney. "What did he have to say?"

John's look remained thoughtful, intense. "Not much." But he seemed to think the idea would work. "Unless United Petroleum wants to play games, I should hear back sometime this afternoon." He tipped back the rim of his hat and glanced down at his watch. "The fact is, I should probably call this morning's ride short and get back to the office in case they contact me this morning."

Judy was aghast. "You don't honestly intend to work, do you? Good heavens, you've been away on an exhausting business trip."

"So?"

"You haven't slept in who knows how long." McFarland's mouth thinned with impatience.

"What's that got to do with anything?"

"Everything," she cried, losing control of her own even temper. She didn't know what was wrong with him this morning, but she had a hunch that a few hours of rest would cure it.

"Just what am I supposed to do?"

"Sleep."

"I'm expecting a phone call."

"Avery will wake you."

"What are you? My nurse?"

Judy's gloved hands tightened around the reins at the unnecessarily harsh edge to his voice. "Someone needs to look after you."

"And I suppose you're volunteering for the job?" McFarland didn't want to shout at her, but he couldn't seem to make himself stop. She was right. God knew he hadn't seen a bed in over forty-eight hours, but he sure as hell didn't want a woman dictating his actions.

Judy clamped her mouth together so tightly that her jaw ached. She refused to rise to the bait of his acid tongue.

They rode together for a half hour without saying a word. McFarland derived little pleasure from the outing. He regretted having snapped at Judy, especially when he would much rather have taken her in his arms and kissed her. He searched his mind for a way to apologize without it costing him his pride, and found none.

When they returned to the stable, Judy lowered herself from Princess's back and turned toward John. "As I recall, only a few hours ago you considered me wise and insightful. I don't know what happened since then, but I really do wish you'd rest."

"Why?"

She clenched her fists. "You're killing yourself working day and night for no reason."

"I call ten million dollars a damn good reason."

"Is it worth your health?" she cried, tears glistening in her eyes. "Is it worth becoming so unreasonable no one can talk to you? Is it worth saying something you don't mean?"

"You seem to be doing a good job of exactly that."

"I care about you."

"Is that supposed to excite me?" he asked. "You care about everything—horses, children . . . bugs. It would be hard to find something that you didn't care about. Listen, Miss Bleeding Heart, I can do without your mollycoddling. Got that?"

"No," she said with incredible pride, her face pale and grim.

"You've been nothing but a damn nuisance since you came to the island. There isn't a man or woman here who doesn't bend to your every wish. Well, I refuse to be one of them. You'll do what I tell you. It won't be the other way around. Have you got that?"

If possible, her face went even paler. Her eyes rounded with pain and shock. She opened her mouth to say something, then closed it again. The effort to restrain the tears drained her of energy. Still, she refused to look away.

"I won't bother you again, John McFarland," she whispered with quiet dignity and turned from him, nearly blinded now by her tears. How quickly everything had changed. She'd missed John until her heart had ached. She'd longed to savor this morning's outing with him and instead had found herself the object of a tongue-lashing she had yet to fully understand.

In her rooms, she sat and stared at the wall as the tears flowed freely down her ashen cheeks. She was in love with a beast. The possibility of ever gaining his heart struck her as ludicrous. In his own words, she was a damn nuisance and, with that, Judy realized that he would probably never have it in him to love her.

At lunchtime, she sent word that she wouldn't be joining him and requested that all her meals be sent to her room. If John found her company so taxing, there was no need to punish him with her presence. She refused to trouble him again and was determined to avoid him until he saw fit to summon her.

A day passed.

A night.

Another day.

Another long, sleepless night.

A third day came and went and still John didn't ask for her. She thought about him, yearned for him. Judy was convinced that she could wilt away in her rooms and he would have cared less. She loved him and he considered her an annoyance. All these weeks when she had treasured every moment with him, he'd found her a bothersome pest.

Still, he didn't summon her. To escape her room, Judy walked along the beach in the early morning light. For the first time she entertained thoughts of leaving and regretfully rejected them. They had struck a bargain, and although it grew increasingly difficult, she would stay on the island until he sent her away.

Countless times Judy wondered why he bothered to keep her there. She yearned to be with her family.

McFarland was growing less amused by the day at Judy's stubbornness. Perhaps he had been a bit unreasonable, but it certainly shouldn't have amounted to this. For four days, she had refused to have anything to do with him. That had been her choice, but enough was enough. The entire house was in an uproar.

McFarland had discovered the chef arguing with Avery. French insults rushed like water out of a spigot while the four-star chef gestured freely with his hands. The entire time, the man sent accusing glances in McFarland's direction.

"What was that all about?" he had asked his assistant later, having found the display only a little short of comical.

"He—ah—is concerned," Avery commented, looking embarrassed and red-faced.

"Concerned? Is it the kitchen help again?"

"No." Avery busied himself with shifting papers around his desk.

"Then what is it?" McFarland pressed.

"He's concerned about Miss Lovin."

McFarland's grin faded and his eyes grew cold. "Judy? What's wrong?"

"He claims she isn't eating properly and that she sends back her meals untouched. He's tempted her with his most famous recipes and nothing seems to work. He fears she is making herself ill."

A muscle jerked convulsively in McFarland's clenched jaw.

"I realize this isn't any of my concern, Mr. McFarland, but . . ."

"You're right, it isn't your business."

Avery squared his shoulders, his own jaw tightening. "I've been with you for several years now, but these last three days have been more difficult than ever. You have been impatient, and unreasonably demanding, and I can find no excuse for it. You have my notice, Mr. McFarland."

McFarland was stunned. Perhaps he had been a bit more demanding in the past few days, but that wasn't any reason for Avery to resign. "As you wish," he answered with some reluctance.

The afternoon went smoothly after that, but when they'd finished, Avery presented him with a brief but precise letter of resignation.

McFarland read it over twice, convinced there must have been some mistake. There wasn't; Avery was leaving him.

In an effort to think through this unexpected turn of events, McFarland took two cold beers from his cooler and decided to visit Sam. To his additional shock, he discovered that the stable man regarded him with a black scowl.

"Don't tell me she's got you on her side as well?" McFarland barked, angry because he should have known better. Judy had had Sam twisted around her little finger from the minute she'd tamed Midnight. "Doesn't a one of you recognize the hand that feeds you? Good Lord, I don't believe it. Not you, too?"

In response, Sam chuckled, ambled to the back of the barn and brought out two rickety chairs.

"Women are a pain in the backside," McFarland said, pulling the tab from the aluminum top and guzzling a long swallow.

Sam joined him in the toast. "Can't say I blame you. You'll do well to be rid of her."

McFarland wiped his mouth with the back of his hand as his bemusement faded. "What do you mean?"

"You don't plan to keep her on the island? Not with the way she's been acting."

McFarland planned exactly that. He had no intention of letting her leave. This thing between them was a spat, nothing more. She'd infringed on his private life and he wouldn't stand for it. Given time, she would recognize the error of her ways and come to him, gushing with apologies. And being the good-hearted soul he was, he would forgive her.

"She's a damn busybody, that one," Sam added. "Why, look at the way she stuck her nose in your affairs, dictating the way you should run your business. No man should be expected to put up with that kind of feminist assertiveness."

"Have you been watching Donohue again?" McFarland felt obligated to ask.

"Look at the way she's constantly needling you, asking for one thing or another, making selfish demands. I hear how she's constantly seeking gifts."

McFarland's face tightened. "She's never asked for a damn thing."

Sam took another long swallow of beer. "If I were you, I'd put her in a rowboat and cast her out of my life. Let her fend for herself. As you said, she's a damn nuisance; she isn't worth the trouble."

McFarland mumbled something unintelligible under his breath. "Who said she was a nuisance?"

"You did, heard you tell her so myself. Should have seen the look in her eyes." Sam's laugh was loud and boisterous. "She's plump full of pride and spirit, that one. You'd best break it if you intend to keep her around here."

It seemed the entire barn had gone still. "What else did I say to her?"

"Oh, lots of things."

"What things?"

The blood drained from McFarland's face as Sam told him. He'd been so exhausted that he didn't remember the half of it. Now, every word, every syllable was a vicious punch to his abdomen.

McFarland crushed the aluminum can with his hands and stood. He felt sick.

"Where are you going?"

McFarland didn't answer.

"You're going to get rid of her, aren't you?" Sam asked, and noting the look on McFarland's face, he chuckled, pleased with himself.

Chapter Seven

Once again McFarland was in the uncomfortable position of needing to seek Judy's forgiveness. It gnawed at his conscience, and clawed at his sleep until he rolled over and stared at the darkened ceiling. His heart constricted and the first doubts concerning what he was doing with Judy surfaced. He'd seen her picture in some newspaper and his interest had been awakened. He had yet to understand what craziness had driven him to force her to come to his island. In the weeks since her arrival his life had been drastically affected. She'd been open, happy, guileless and unbelievably gentle when she had every excuse to hate him. He had berated her, lashed out at her, and still she turned those incredible eyes on him and found it within her to smile.

By everything that was right, he should release her and send her back to her family. His heart pounded slowly, painfully, at the thought of never hearing the sound of her laughter again, or having those incredible round eyes smile into his, or seeing her ride across his land with her hair in careless disarray. A heaviness pressed against his chest.

He couldn't do it—sending her away was unthinkable. The tenderness in her eyes and her gentle smile filled him with an exhilaration he couldn't begin to analyze. He wasn't entirely sure he wanted to. She was an angel who caused him to feel things he'd never experienced, emotions he'd fought against most of his life. All he knew was that he needed her on St. Steven's for now. He'd deal with tomorrow later.

Judy pounded the feather pillow and battled with another wave of depression. She was wide awake. In another hour it would be dawn and she could escape the self-imposed prison of her room. With nothing better to do, she climbed out of bed, dressed and crept out of the house, heading for the stables.

Her heart felt incredibly weary.

The sky remained dark, but the promise of dawn lay just over the horizon. She could hear Sam stirring in the back of the barn as she saddled Princess and rode toward the beach.

Sam's features were twisted in a dark scowl as he searched McFarland's face in the half light of early dawn.

"She's gone," he announced harshly.

"Who?"

"Princess."

McFarland's eyes widened. No one would dare steal the mare. Only Judy rode her. "Has anyone checked the house to see . . ."

"The maid says there's no one in her room. Her bed barely looks slept in."

McFarland's own features hardened with sharp determination, and in a single motion, he swung his weight onto Midnight's back. He braced his knees against the stallion's powerful sides and pulled tightly on the reins. "In which direction does she usually ride?"

Sam gestured widely with both hands. "North. Sometimes east."

"I'll head west."

Sam's nod was curt, his eyes boring into McFarland's. "You bring her back; she belongs here."

The words were shouted as McFarland raced out of the yard. He wouldn't come back until he found her. By God, he would horsewhip the one who had helped her in this underhanded scheme. What the hell good was security if she could carry out her own escape? He'd fire the whole damn lot of them, but first he had to find Judy.

McFarland would have ridden from one side of the island to the other, torn down the entire jungle to stop her. To his utter astonishment, all it took was a wild fifteen-minute ride. He came upon her with such shocking ease that his heart begun to slam against his chest. He paused, his frantic heartbeat stilling as he raised his eyes to the sky in eternal gratitude.

She was walking on the beach with Princess following two steps behind. Her head drooped lackadaisically; the reins were draped over her shoulders as she ambled along. Although McFarland was positioned high on the ridge above, he could see how distressed Judy was. Her head hung low, her shoulders were hunched and it looked as though a steel mantle were weighing heavily upon her shoulders. He didn't need to see her tear-streaked face to know that she had been crying. The realization had the oddest effect upon him. Guilt tore at him and his chest tightened, constricting with a pain that was razor sharp. He couldn't take his eyes off her. Witnessing her pain brought out such an overwhelming desire to protect her that he could hardly breathe.

Since the night Sam had set him straight about the things he'd said to Judy, McFarland had sought for a means of salvaging his pride. He admitted he owed her an apology, but he yearned to give it without denting his considerable pride. He could present her with a token gift, perhaps. Something that would convey his message and cost him little emotionally. Watching her now, a sick feeling settled into the pit of his stomach and he realized he would gladly fall to his knees and beg her forgiveness. He was a selfish bastard and Beauty—his Beauty—deserved far better.

Judy wiped the moisture from her cheek, angry with herself for being so melancholy. From the first, she had known it would be difficult to love John. She'd thought she'd accepted that. In the long days since their ride together, she had come to understand far better the cost love demanded. But she had her pride, too—in some ways it was as considerable as John's—and she would die before she would let him know that he held her heart in the palm of his hand.

A flash of ebony caught her attention and she turned and spotted John on the ridge above her. Judy's heart rushed to her throat. He pulled on the reins and she realized with a start that he was planning on meeting her. It was one thing to realize he had found her, and another to allow him to see her tears.

Desperate to escape, she mounted Princess and slapped the reins hard against the mare's flanks. Princess shot across the beach, her powerful hind feet kicking up a flurry of sand. Judy realized her best chance of escape was in the jungle and headed in that direction. Chancing a look behind her, she was astonished to see that John had already reached the beach.

"Hurry, Princess," she cried, frantically whipping the reins back and forth across her neck.

Judy didn't see what it was that darted across the beach, but Princess reared, her legs kicking in terror. Unable to stop herself, Judy slipped sideways in the saddle. In a desperate effort to regain her balance, she groped for the saddle horn, but it was too difficult to keep atop the bucking horse. A sense of unreality filled her. She hadn't been unseated by a horse since she was a child. She refused to believe it, but the ground that rushed up to meet her was more than real. A cry of panic froze in her lungs as she lifted her arms to break the fall. Then the impact of her torso against the solid beach brutally drove the air from her lungs and for a moment everything went black.

McFarland saw Princess buck and watched helplessly as Judy teetered while frantically trying to regain her seat. He saw her fall and knew she'd landed hard. A score of swear words scorched the morning mist and his heart thundered with alarm. The thoughts that flashed through his mind were completely illogical. He'd sell his business interests around the world if she were unhurt. If that didn't satisfy the powers that be, he offered his life, his heart, his soul—anything—just as long as Judy wasn't hurt.

He pulled Midnight to an abrupt halt, vaulted from the stallion's back and ran across the sand, more frightened than he could remember being in his life.

Falling to his knees at Judy's side, he gently rolled her over. The steady, even pulsing at the side of her neck caused him to go weak with relief. He ripped the jacket from his arms and placed it under her head. Then, not knowing what else to do, he lifted her limp hand into his own, frantically rubbing the inside of her wrist.

Judy's eyes fluttered open to discover John leaning over her, looking sickly pale. "Princess?" she whispered, and tried to sit up.

It took McFarland a moment to realize she was worried about the mare. He was astonished; Judy could have been maimed, or worse, killed, and she seemed to care nothing for her own well-being.

"Is she hurt?"

McFarland shook his head and responded in a husky voice. "She's fine. What about you?"

Her smile was little more than a slight trembling of her lips. It was too soon to tell. She felt like she was going to throw up and the world spun crazily. "I'm all right," she said weakly, putting up a brave front.

"You're sure?" His intense gaze burned over her face.

"The only thing bruised is my pride." With some difficulty she stood, stumbled and swayed toward him. Her ribs hurt like crazy, but she successfully hid the pain.

McFarland caught her, gently wrapping his arms around her, holding her against him, grateful for the excuse to bring her into the shelter of his embrace. He brushed the hair away from her face, and Judy noted that he was shaking as much as she was.

"I'm fine, John. Something must have spooked Princess. I think it was a rabbit." She tilted her head back and saw the torment in his eyes as he relived the moment of her fall.

Their gazes met. Neither moved; neither breathed. Slowly, he lowered his mouth to hers. The kiss was gentle and savage at the same time. Judy could find no way to describe the turbulent sensation that jolted her. It was as though she realized she could have been killed and forever denied the feel of John's arms again. Judy wanted to cherish this moment forever, and forget the pain.

They remained locked in each other's arms long after the kiss had ended. Timeless seconds passed, each more precious that the one before.

"I've got to get you to a doctor," he said at last.

"John, I'll be all right."

"You're shaking."

She smiled, unable to tell him his kisses contributed to the trembling as much as the pain.

His low whistle brought Midnight to their side. "You'll ride with me."

"But . . ."

One look effectively cut off any argument. McFarland climbed onto Midnight's back first.

Judy stared at the stallion and felt her knees go weak. The last thing she wanted to do was get back on a horse. Although she strove to reassure John that she was unhurt, she felt as though someone had taken a baseball bat to her ribs. It hurt to breathe and she ached everywhere. Nothing seemed broken, but something wasn't right, either. "What if he won't seat me?" she asked shakily.

John dismissed that suggestion with a curious smile. "You said yourself Midnight was your friend."

"So I did," she grumbled, staring at the hand he offered her. She accepted it, and his strong fingers closed over her own, prepared to lift her onto the stallion's back. However, the simple action of raising her arm caused her to gasp with pain.

Hurriedly, she drew it back to her side, closed her eyes and pressed her forehead against John's leg. The next thing she knew, she was on her knees in the sand, clenching her side.

"You idiot," he shouted, dismounting, "why didn't you say something?"

Tears welled in her eyes as she lifted her pain-riddled gaze to his. "Why do you always yell at me?" she asked in a hoarse whisper.

"Beauty, I'm sorry."

She held her arm protectively across her ribs. "Only my father calls me that."

"It's true, you know," he said gently, kneeling beside her, holding her with such tenderness that she couldn't identify the greater pain—loving John or the ache in her ribs.

"I'm not beautiful," she countered.

"Yes, love, you are. You're the most beautiful woman I know. Now, don't argue with me, understand?"

She offered him a weak smile.

The trip back to the house seemed to take torturous hours. She pleaded with him to leave her and send someone back for her. The injury wasn't so bad that she couldn't stand to be alone for a half hour or more. John adamantly refused and, in the end, she did ride Midnight, cradled in John's arms so that he absorbed every jolt and shock.

She rode sidesaddle, her head resting against his chest, her arms around his middle. Their progress was slow and by the time they arrived she was hazy with pain and incredibly sleepy.

Sam and several others rushed out to greet them.

"Send for a doctor," John barked urgently.

With some effort, Judy lifted her head. "I thought you said you weren't going to yell anymore."

"I said that?" He pretended to be amazed.

She frowned and drew in a slow, painful breath. "Maybe you didn't, at that."

His fingers found the back of her neck and he buried them deep in her hair. "If it will make the hurt go away, I'll promise never to raise my voice again."

The ache in her side immediately lessened.

He issued other orders, but in a subdued voice that swelled Judy's heart, not because she found his shouting objectionable, but because he cared enough about her to try to please her. After the last four days of the bitter cold war that had raged between them, this sweet attention was bliss.

John helped her off Midnight's back and carried her into the house. She protested when he started up the stairs to her room, but it didn't stop him.

"I'm too heavy," she cried.

"Now look who's yelling."

"John, please, you're the one who'll need the doctor if you insist on hauling me up these stairs."

"I'll risk it."

"But I wish you wouldn't." It was useless to protest. Besides, he was already halfway up the staircase.

When he reached the hallway outside her room, he kicked her door open, crossed the room and gently laid her on the bed. It took Judy only an instant to realize that lying down wasn't the thing to do and kicking out her feet, she struggled to a sitting position.

"What's wrong?" McFarland saw the flash of pain in her eyes and felt it as strongly as if the agony were his own.

She shook her head and closed her eyes. "Nothing. Just go away, will you? I'll be fine in a minute."

To her surprise he did leave her, but two maids were in her room within a matter of seconds. They were followed by the security guard who had met her the day of her arrival.

Judy grinned. "So we meet again."

"I have some medical training," he explained. "Mr. McFarland asked that I check you over before the doctor arrives."

Judy nodded and slumped onto the end of her bed.

McFarland was pacing in the hallway outside her room when Wilson returned. "Well?" he asked anxiously.

"My guess is that she's cracked a couple of ribs."

"She's in considerable pain, isn't she?" Although Judy tried to hide it from him, McFarland could tell that she wanted to scream and her agony burned in his veins, scorching his conscience and searing his tormented soul.

"She's pretending it doesn't hurt, but I know better," Wilson commented wryly.

"Give her something for the pain," McFarland demanded gruffly.

"How is Miss Lovin, sir?" the chef asked as he bravely stepped forward.

Only a day before McFarland would have bitten off the pompous man's head for daring to approach him on a subject that was none of his concern. Now he patiently explained the extent of Judy's injuries and answered his and the others' legion of questions.

From there McFarland went to his offices. Avery stood when he entered the room.

Before his assistant could ask, he rattled off his now rehearsed report. "Cracked ribs, bruises and a mild concussion. She'll be confined to her bed for a few days and good as new in a couple of months. Or so the doctor claims."

Avery nodded. "How about you?"

"Me?"

"It doesn't appear to me that you're going to recover in a couple of months," he said boldly.

McFarland paled and glared at his assistant before walking into his office and soundly closing the door. Avery was right; McFarland doubted that he'd ever be the same again. He had been shaken to the very roots of his existence. He buried his face in his hands and sat, unmoving, for what seemed like hours.

Somehow he made it through the day, dictating memos, making decisions, charting the course of financial institutions, but for the little emotion he put into it, he could have been playing Monopoly. Nothing seemed real; nothing seemed right.

The mere thought of food nauseated him.

The other man looked uncertain for the first time. "I don't know that I should, Mr. McFarland. The doctor might want to . . ."

"It could be hours before he arrives. Give her something and do it now. That's an order."

Wilson nodded, swallowing any argument. "Right away."

He returned a few minutes later with two capsules, instructing Judy to take them both. Within minutes she drifted into a troubled sleep. She curled into a tight ball, taking shallow breaths in an effort to minimize the pain.

When she woke, she discovered that John was sitting at her bedside, staring at his hands, his face bleak, his eyes lifeless.

"John?"

He straightened and turned toward her. "Yes, love?"

"The island needs . . . something. A medical facility. What if one of the children were to get hurt? Then . . . what? There's nowhere . . ." She felt so sluggish, so miserable. The pills hadn't taken the pain way; only her mind was numb.

"The doctor will be here soon," he hurried to assure her.

She nodded and moistened her lips with her tongue. "I'm thirsty."

"Here." He lifted her head and held a glass of cool water to her lips. She managed to take several sips. When she had finished drinking, he gently kissed her forehead.

"John?" Her voice was little more than a slurred whisper. She struggled to keep her eyes open and gave up the effort.

The soft catch in her voice stabbed at his heart. "Yes, love."

"I'm sorry to be such a nuisance."

The words burned him like a red-hot iron. "You were never that."

"But you said . . ."

He gripped her hand in his own and raised it to his lips, tenderly kissing her knuckles. "I was wrong." McFarland couldn't remember ever admitting that to anyone.

He stayed at her bedside until the medical team arrived. Then he lingered outside her room until the physician had finished the examination, which seemed to take hours. McFarland paced the area in front of her room so long that he grew dizzy. He smoked rarely, but desperately needed a cigarette.

His thoughts ran into each other until they flashed through his mind in a muddled sequence. Judy running away from him, Judy falling, Judy in pain. It was all his fault. Lord knew he had never meant to hurt her. She was too delicate, too sweet to bear the brunt of his brutality.

When the physician finally did appear, McFarland found himself studying the other man, fearing what he would soon learn. "Will she be all right?" His eyes pleaded with the white-haired man for assurance.

"I believe so. We brought along a portable X machine. She's cracked two ribs and has a slight cussion."

"Any internal damage?" That was McFarlan greatest fear.

"Not that we can detect."

He ran his fingers through his hair. "Should she be hospitalized?"

The middle-aged physician with the stocky build shook his head. "I can't see where that would do any good. What she needs now more than anything is rest. For the time being she isn't going to feel much like getting out of bed. However, that's for the best. Let her sleep."

"How long?"

"Keep her down a couple of days, then gradually increase her activity."

"What about the pain? I don't want her to suffer." He couldn't bear to see her face twisted in agony.

"I've left a prescription and instructions with my nurse, Miss Reinholt. Miss Lovin is sleeping comfortably now."

McFarland let out his breath in a long, slow sigh. "Good. Thank you, doctor." He offered the physician his hand and had Wilson escort the medical team to the waiting helicopter.

McFarland checked on Judy one last time before heading toward his office. He was stalled in the foyer by several of the staff members. They raised questioning eyes to him, their concern evident.

couldn't eat; he couldn't work. And when night came, he discovered he couldn't sleep, either. He'd tried to stay away, to let her rest, and realized it was impossible.

The nurse in the stiff white uniform answered his knock on Judy's door.

"She's sleeping."

McFarland nodded, feeling foolish. "Go ahead and take a break, I'll stay with her."

The woman looked grateful, and left soon afterward.

McFarland was thankful to spend the time alone with Judy. Her face was relaxed now and revealed no signs of pain. That eased the load of guilt that had burdened him from the moment he had watched Judy slide helplessly from the mare's back.

He couldn't tolerate the thought of her in pain. He wasn't squeamish, never had been, but Judy's whimper had had the most curious effect upon him. He had gone weak. With others, McFarland had often battled feelings of rage; with Judy he could only blame himself. He felt sick with his guilt.

"John." His name was little more than a faint whisper.

"I'm here." Anxiously, he scooted the chair to her bedside.

The clock on the nightstand said it was near midnight. Or was it noon? Judy didn't know anymore. Everything remained so fuzzy and unclear in her mind. "Have you been here all this time?"

"No." He shook his head. "The nurse needed a break."

"The nurse?"

"Yes, the doctor felt you needed around-the-clock attention."

"That's ridiculous." She tried to laugh and sucked in a harsh breath, her ribs heartily protesting.

"Sh, you're suppose to keep quiet."

She ignored that and pushed herself up on one elbow. "Help me sit up, would you?"

"No."

"John, please, I need to talk to you."

"No, you don't."

"I'm on my deathbed, remember? Humor me." He grudgingly helped her into a sitting position.

Next he fluffed up her pillow and securely tucked the sheets around her waist.

A smile lit up her eyes and for the life of him, McFarland couldn't tear his gaze away. "There," he said, proudly, brushing his palms against each other several times as though he had accomplished some amazing feat.

"What's that?" Judy pointed toward a small crate on the floor next to the dresser.

"A gift."

"From whom?"

"Me."

Although it required some effort, she managed a smile. "Well, for heaven's sake, bring it to me."

He lifted it from the crate after breaking away the

rugged strips of wood. It was cradled in a thick blanket. "I meant to have it wrapped, all frilly with bows, the way you'd like."

"Oh, John, it doesn't matter. As it is, I don't understand why you'd want to buy me anything."

The room went quiet as McFarland reclaimed his chair. "Go ahead and open it."

The object was heavy and awkward in her lap. With infinite care, Judy unrolled the blanket, her excitement growing. As the bronze figure became recognizable, she paused and raised her eyes to his. "John? Oh, John, could it be what I think it is?"

He arched both eyebrows playfully. "I don't know."

Tears filled her eyes and Judy bit her bottom lip, too overcome to speak.

"Judy?"

She pressed her fingers to her mouth as she blinked back the tears. "It's the Riordan sculpture Mother gave Father. He was forced to sell it . . . recently."

"Yes."

"You knew?" Her hand lovingly traced the bronze piece, stroking it as though she hadn't believed that she would ever hold it in her hands again.

Reverently, she set the sculpture aside and lifted her arms to John. Tears glistened in her eyes. "Come here," she whispered brokenly. "I want to thank you."

Chapter Eight

McFarland made excuses to visit Judy. Ten times a day he found reasons that demanded he go to her. He discovered it was necessary to confer with her nurse at least twice a day, sometimes three times. He delivered Judy's lunch along with his own so they could share their meals together. In the evening, he felt Miss Reinholt, the nurse, should have some time off, so McFarland took it upon himself to stay with the patient. Seldom did he come empty-handed. Judy's injury was the perfect excuse for him to give her the things he felt she deserved.

Judy's eyes would light up with such happiness at his arrival that each day his excuses became all the more flimsy. The Riordan sculpture rested on the nightstand and more than once McFarland had caught Judy gazing at it longingly. He knew the piece reminded her of her life in New York, but she never mentioned leaving the island. Nor did he.

"John," Judy whispered the third day of her convalescence. "You have got to get rid of that woman." She bobbed her head in the direction of the stiff-backed nurse who sat knitting in the opposite corner of the room.

"Why?" He lowered his voice conspiratorially, his eyes twinkling.

"I'm not joking, so quit laughing at me! Miss Reinholt is driving me batty. Every time I turn around she's flashing a light in my eyes or placing a thermometer under my tongue. When I complained, she suggested there were other areas where she could stick the blasted thing."

Despite himself, McFarland burst into laughter. Judy's eyes narrowed and she whispered gruffly, "I'm pleased you find this so amusing."

"I'm sorry," he said, but he didn't feel the least bit contrite.

In a huff, Judy crossed her arms over her chest and tried to be angry with him. She couldn't. He'd been so wonderful, so attentive, that it wasn't in her to find fault with him. It was as though he yearned to make up to her for his harshness since her arrival on the island.

"I'm sick of sitting in bed." She tried to appear stern, but the edges of her mouth quivered with suppressed laughter.

He grinned and nodded.

"You'd think I was the only woman ever to survive two cracked ribs—the way everyone's acting. I've got news for you. I am not a medical marvel."

"I realize that."

"You don't," she countered, struggling to keep her voice low and unemotional. "Otherwise you'd let me up."

"You're allowed to get up."

"Sure, for five minutes every hour. Big deal." She stuck out her arm. "I'm losing my tan! I'll have you know I worked hard for this."

He chuckled and Judy resisted the urge to stick her elbow into his ribs. He seemed to find the entire situation comical.

"You aren't taking me seriously, John, and it's driving me crazy!"

"All right, all right. I'll tell Miss Reinholt that you're allowed to get up more often."

"I want to sit in the sun," she pleaded.

"Perhaps tomorrow."

It would do little good to argue. "Promise?"

He nodded. His eyes held hers and were so warm and caressing that Judy wondered why she ever longed for sunshine when she had John.

"And . . ."

"Hmm?"

"No more gifts." Her room was filled to overflowing with everything he'd given her. There was hardly available space for all the flowers—roses, orchids, daisies. In addition, he'd given her bottle upon bottle of expensive French perfumes, and jewelry until she swore she could open her own franchise. Her slightest wish had been fulfilled ten times over.

"I like giving you things."

Her hand reached for his. Intuitively Judy recognized that John was soothing his conscience. A troubled frown lined her forehead. It was important that he know she didn't blame him. "The accident wasn't your fault."

His fingers grasped hers and his face tightened. "I caused you to fall . . ."

"John, no." Her free hand caressed his clenched jaw. "I was the one who ran from you. It was an accident." In her heart, the pain of her cracked ribs was a small price to pay for an end to the hostility between them.

Miss Reinholt set her needlework aside and checked her watch. "It's time to take Miss Lovin's temperature," she announced in a crisp, professional tone.

"See what I mean?" Judy said out of the side of her mouth.

"I'd better get back to the office." John leaned over and lightly brushed his lips over hers, then stood and left the room.

Obediently, Judy opened her mouth as the nurse approached. She lay back and closed her eyes, savoring the memory of those few minutes with John. Although he came often, he seldom stayed more than ten or fifteen minutes. Judy was so pleased to see him for any amount of time that she didn't complain.

John wasn't her only visitor. Avery Andersen arrived shortly after noon, pulled up a chair and talked for an hour. He was such a fuddy-duddy that Judy had to struggle to keep from laughing. He wasn't any taller than she and couldn't seem to finish a sentence without stuttering. Toward the end of their conversation, he seemed to relax.

Ten minutes after Avery's visit, John reappeared, looking perplexed. He ran his fingers through his hair and studied her. "What did you say to Avery?"

"When?"

"Just now. He was here, wasn't he?"

Judy nodded. "I didn't say anything special. He came to see how I was doing. You didn't mind, did you? I mean, if he should have been doing something else, I apologize."

John's look was absent as he shook his head. "We'd finished for the day."

"Is something wrong?"

John smiled then, a rich, rare smile. "He's decided to stay."

"Avery? I didn't know he was leaving."

"He isn't," he muttered, bemused. "At least, not anymore."

"Well, I'm pleased if you are."

He stared at her. "You're sure you didn't say anything?"

"I said a lot of things."

His gaze returned to her. "Like what?"

"John, honestly. I don't know . . . I mentioned the weather and we talked about the stock market—he was far more knowledgeable about the subject than I'll ever be. We talked about you some, but only a little bit. Now that you mention it, he did seem overly nervous at first."

"Avery's always nervous."

"Then there was nothing out of the ordinary."

McFarland sat on the edge of the bed and braced his hands on either side of her head. "It appears I'm in your debt again."

"Good, I like it that way."

He looked as though he wanted to kiss her. He even bent his head closer to her own, his gaze centered on her lips. Judy wished he would and tried to beckon him with her eyes, but he didn't and left soon afterward, leaving her frustrated and more than a little disappointed. He had kissed her several times since the accident, light kisses that teased her with the memory of other more potent ones. He treated her more like an indulgent older brother. Infuriated, she was powerless to change his attitude until she was out of bed.

Disappointed, Judy crossed her arms over her chest and sighed dejectedly. She couldn't blame John for not finding her tempting; she must look a sight with her plain nightgowns. What she wouldn't give for a skimpy piece of silk!

Feeling tired, Judy slept for the next hour and woke to distant hammering, at least that was what it sounded like. The tap, tap, tap was so faint that she was astonished that she even heard it.

"What's that noise?" She sat upright, looking toward her nurse.

"Is it troubling you? Mr. McFarland instructed me to let him know if the construction disturbed your rest."

"Construction?"

"Yes, Mr. McFarland is having a medical clinic built. I'll be staying on the island full-time following your recovery."

"He's building a clinic?"

"Yes, I've already seen several of the children for physical examinations. Arrangements are being made to fly a doctor in twice a week from now on."

Judy was too astonished to make a sound. Stinging tears filled her eyes. Grimacing at the pain, Judy tossed aside the sheets and climbed out of bed. She reached for the robe that lay at the foot of her bed.

"Miss Lovin, what are you doing?"

She wiped the tears from her face and tried to speak, but couldn't. Instead, she shook her head, and, holding her hand against her side, walked out of her room.

"Just where do you think you're going?" Virginia Reinholt demanded, hands pressed against her overly round hips.

It was all Judy could do to point down the stairs.

"Miss Lovin, I must insist that you return to your room immediately. Mr. McFarland will be most displeased."

Judy ignored the woman and carefully moved down the stairs, taking one step at a time. It hurt to walk, but she discovered that pressing her arm against her side lessened the ache.

The middle-aged nurse ran ahead of Judy and was waiting for her at the bottom of the stairs. "I must insist you return to your room this instant."

"No," Judy said with as much resolve as she could muster.

"Then you leave me no option but to inform my

employer." The nurse marched toward McFarland's suite of offices.

The flustered woman was standing in front of Avery's desk, visibly displeased when Judy appeared. Avery wiped his forehead with his handkerchief, straightened his bow tie and nodded now and again.

Judy sidestepped them both, knocked politely on John's door and let herself into his office.

"Judy?" He rose to his feet immediately. "Good God, woman, what are you trying to do? Kill yourself?" He noted her tears then, and lowered his voice sufficiently. "Love, what is it?" He walked around his desk and pulled her into his arms.

Judy tried to tell him, but her voice refused to cooperate. Whimpering softly, she framed his face with her hands and spread a foray of kisses over his jaw and cheeks, quick, random kisses. Unerringly, she found his eyes, his nose, his ear. She kissed him again and again, ignoring his weak protests.

"Judy," he said thickly, his hands on her upper arms.

He continued to speak, but Judy effectively cut him off by slanting her mouth over his, thanking him silently for his thoughtfulness. Eagerly, her lips parted moist under his, and the first sensuous taste of his mouth stilled her.

Gently, McFarland forced her mouth open wider. The intensity of the kiss rocked them both and, feeling weak, he found a chair and sat with her nestled in his lap.

He drew her closer and teased her with feathery strokes of his tongue. Judy moaned, lost in the whirling sensation.

McFarland had restrained from holding or touching her like this. Her innocence humbled him, and he feared he would frighten her with the fierce passion she aroused in him.

Since the accident, he'd kissed her a handful of times, but each gentle kiss had only created more of a need than it satisfied. Now her tongue boldly met his own, dueling, probing deeper and deeper, stroking and exploring. McFarland trembled uncontrollably like a leaf trapped in the wind. His need for her mounted with such intensity that it sapped the strength from him. Her unrestrained breasts were full and ripe against his chest and it was another torture not to fill his hands with them and know for himself the feel of her silken skin against his own. Emotions that had been hiding just below the surface gushed forth, nearly overpowering him with their intensity.

Groaning, McFarland tore his mouth free and nuzzled his face in her neck, holding her as close as he dared, afraid of causing her further pain. Her tenderness enveloped him, and with it a desire so overwhelming that he couldn't hold her much longer and remain sane.

"John," she pleaded, "don't stop."

"Oh, Lord . . ." He kissed her again because refusing her anything was beyond him. His mouth

142

ardently claimed hers, and when he'd finished, their breathing was staggered and weak.

Gently, he held her face and wiped the tears from her cheek with the side of his thumb, still aghast at the power she held over him. "What happened?"

She shook her head. "I heard pounding . . . or what I thought was . . . pounding."

McFarland nodded, encouraging her to continue. "You're building a medical clinic?"

"Yes."

She brushed her hands over his face, stroking, savoring every inch of his beloved features while she gathered her composure. "Thank you," she said in a small, broken voice.

McFarland studied her, more perplexed than ever. He'd given her a host of gifts, but nothing had evoked this response. Not even the sculpture. A simple medical clinic had reduced her to tears.

A hard knock forced them apart.

"I must apologize for this rude interruption, Mr. McFarland," the nurse said, standing just inside the door, looking angry and frustrated. "There was no stopping her—I did try."

"I flew the coop," Judy whispered, and was rewarded with a quick smile from John.

"I really must insist that she return to bed immediately."

"Oh, do I have to?" Judy asked with a ragged sigh.

McFarland stood, bringing Judy with him. "Yes, you must."

"Another day of this and you might as well bury me in my jammies." Playfully, she pressed the back of her hand to her forehead and rolled her eyes.

"Another kiss like that," McFarland said, low enough for only Judy to hear, "and you can bury me, too."

Virginia Reinholt led the way back to Judy's room, clucking as she went, listing Judy's myriad faults with each step.

Judy looked into John's eyes as he carried her, letting him know who was really the injured party as far as her nurse went.

McFarland followed Miss Reinholt into the room and gently lowered Judy to the bed. She didn't release her arms from around his neck, but held him a moment longer while she whispered, "Just wait until you get sick!"

"Are you sure you're up to this?" McFarland asked for the fifth time in as many minutes. The thought of her on another horse made him wince.

"If you ask me that one more time I think I'll scream," Judy told him with a scathing look that added credence to her threat. "It's been three weeks since the accident. I'm not recovering from brain surgery, you know!"

"But horseback riding . . ."

"If Miss Reinholt approved, so can you. Besides, I want to ride again before I lose my nerve."

"To hell with yours," McFarland muttered, "mine is shot."

Sam brought both Princess and Midnight around to the front of the stables and held Princess while Judy slipped her foot into the stirrup and mounted the mare.

The effort caused a painful twinge, but nothing she wasn't able to readily disguise. "There," she said triumphantly.

"Right." McFarland swung his weight atop Midnight and circled the yard. She hadn't fooled him; she was hurting and he was furious that she wouldn't put this off longer until she'd had the time to heal completely.

"Are you coming or not?" She tossed the question over her shoulder as she trotted ahead of him toward the beach.

"Judy, for God's sake, slow down," he shouted, racing after her.

"No."

The wind carried her laughter and McFarland relaxed in his saddle as the sound washed over him like a healing balm. The last few weeks had drastically altered their relationship.

He had never had a time like this with a woman. A shared look could mean more than an hour's conversation; a kiss in the moonlight could fill him with longing for her. She might have been innocent, but she aroused in him a sensual awareness far stronger than anything he'd ever known. When she laughed, he laughed; when she ached, he ached; when she was happy, he was happy.

He spent as much of his day with her as his business would allow. For the first time, he delegated his duties freely. He'd known that Avery Andersen was a competent manager, but in the past three weeks, he'd learned to fully utilize and appreciate the man's instinctive talents.

If McFarland needed to read over papers regarding his business interests, he would often do it in the evenings. Content simply to be at his side, Judy would sit across from him in the library reading, a book propped in front of her, while he handled his affairs. Oftentimes he found his interest wavering. Watching her was by far the greater joy.

There had been a time when he would have despaired of taking off an afternoon; now he dedicated days to Judy. She was like a multifaceted jewel that sparkled with each twist and turn. Judy Lovin was his jewel, his light . . . his Beauty.

McFarland couldn't imagine his life without her now. Her laughter filled his days; her smile touched his soul. Some inner, spiritual part of himself must have known this would happen—that was the only possible explanation for why he had forced her to come to the island. For the first time in his life he was utterly content. There were no more mountains to conquer, no more bridges to cross. There was nothing he desired more than what he possessed right at that moment.

"I've missed this," Judy said happily, breaking into his thoughts.

He'd ridden only five or six times himself, preferring to spend any free time with her.

"John," she said, her voice softening, "I thought I specifically asked you to stop buying me gifts."

"I vaguely recall something to that effect," he said, feeling glib.

"If you think you've fooled me, you're wrong. I know exactly what's been going on."

"I wouldn't dream of disregarding your wishes." He did his best to disguise a smile.

"I suppose you don't think I've noticed the way Sam's been walking around like a peacock. You've bought another horse."

The woman was a marvel. Shaking his head, McFarland chuckled. "She's a beauty. You're going to love her."

"Oh, John, honestly. What am I going to do with you?" *Love me. Marry me. Give me children. Fill my life with joy and laughter.* The possibilities were endless.

"Oh, John, look," Judy cried. "The children are playing in the surf."

McFarland paused, watched their antics and laughed.

"They haven't seen you in a couple of weeks," he said after a moment. "I'll wait for you here."

"Wait for me?" She turned questioning eyes to him.

"I'll frighten them away."

Judy frowned. She understood what he meant, but it was time the children got to know him the way she

147

did, the way he really was. "But you're with me," she explained, climbing down from Princess. "Come on." She held her hand out to him.

McFarland felt a twinge of nervousness as he joined her. He hadn't been around children much and if he were to admit it, he would tell her that he felt as apprehensive as they did.

"Philippe. Elizabeth." Judy called their names and watched as they turned, paused only a moment, then raced toward her.

"Judy!"

Arms went flying around her amidst a chorus of happy cries.

Judy fell to her knees and joyously hugged each one.

"We heard you nearly died."

"There's a nurse on the island now. Did you know that?"

"Paulo got a new tooth."

"It'll take more than a fall to do me in," she told them with a light laugh, dismissing their concern. She raised her eyes to John's, daring him to contradict her. "Children, I have someone I want you to meet." She rose to her feet and slipped her arm around John's waist. "This is Mr. McFarland. He owns the island."

All the children froze until Elizabeth and Margaret curtsied formally, their young faces serious as they confronted John McFarland. The boys bowed then, tucking their arms around their waists.

McFarland frowned, raised his brows at Judy and followed the boys' example, bending in half. "I'm most pleased to make your acquaintance."

"Did you build us the school?"

"The nurse stuck a needle in my arm, but I didn't cry."

"The doctor said I have to eat my vegetables."

The flurry of activity took him by surprise. Patiently, he was introduced to each child.

"Judy. Judy." Jimmy came running from the edge of the jungle, carrying a huge cage. "Did you see my bird?"

The youth was so obviously proud of his catch that Judy paid undue attention to the large blue parrot. "He's lovely."

"I caught him myself," Jimmy went on to explain. "He was trapped in the brush and I grabbed him and put him inside the cage."

The square box had been woven from palm leaves. "You did an excellent job."

"He sings, too. Every morning."

"I think you should set him free," Margaret said, slipping her hand into Judy's. "No one's happy in a cage."

"But he sings," Jimmy countered.

"He's such a pretty bird," Philippe said, sticking his finger into the holes, hoping the parrot would jump on it. Instead, his wings fluttered madly in an effort to escape.

"I give him food. He'll even let me hold him."

"But how do you know that he's happy?" Margaret persisted.

"Because I just do!"

"But how do you know he'll be happy tomorrow?"

"Because he will!"

Judy felt the blood drain from her face. The happy chatter of the children sharply abated. Even the ocean appeared to hold back the surf. Judy couldn't take her eyes from the blue parrot. Her throat clogged with emotion. She was like that bird. Against her will, she had been trapped into coming to the island. John had forced her into leaving everything she loved behind. He had given her gift upon gift, petted her, held her in high regard, but it had changed nothing. She was still in a cage, a gilded one, but nevertheless a cage. She could flutter her wings, wanting to escape, but she was trapped as effectively as the parrot.

"I . . . think I should get back to the house," she said, her voice shaky and weak.

"It was too much for you," John grumbled, taking her by the elbow and leading her back to Princess. "You've gone pale," he said gently, studying her.

Judy felt as though someone had robbed her of her happiness. She'd been playing a fool's game to believe that she could ever be more than a plaything to John. He had told her when she first arrived that she had been brought to St. Steven's to amuse him. She'd fulfilled that expectation well, so content was she with her surroundings.

The ride back to the house seemed to require all her energy.

"I'm contacting the doctor," McFarland announced the minute they had dismounted and the horses had been led away. "I knew it was too soon, but I went against my better judgment."

"No," Judy said, hardly able to look at him. "I'll go lie down for a moment. Then I'll be fine." She knew that wasn't true, but she needed an excuse to get away from him and think. She doubted that she'd ever be the same again.

A letter was waiting for her on the dresser in her room. She stared at the familiar handwriting and felt overwhelmingly homesick. Tears burned for release as she held the envelope to her breast and closed her eyes. Home. Her father. David. New York had never seemed so far from her, or so unattainable.

The content of the letter had an even more curious effect upon her. Suddenly in control of herself again, she marched out of her room and down the stairs to confront John.

He was in his office dictating letters to Avery when she approached him. He looked up, surprised to find her standing here. "Judy," he said softly. "Are you feeling better?"

"I'm fine." She noted how he smiled blithely, unaware of the change in her spirit. "John, I need to talk to you."

He dismissed Avery with a shake of his head. Judy closed the door after his assistant and turned to face him, pressing her hands against the door. Her lack of emotion surprised even her.

"There was a letter from my family in my room when I returned."

"I'd heard one had been delivered."

She dropped her hands to her side. "My brother is getting married."

McFarland grinned, pleased the other man had found someone who would share his life. "It seems the shipping business has improved." With a little subtle help from him. The Lovins need never know, and it eased his conscience to repay them in small measure for sending Judy to him.

"My father is happy with his choice and so am I. David has loved Marie for several years now, but delayed the wedding because . . . well, you know why."

For having received such good news, Judy didn't appear happy.

"John," she said, boldly meeting his gaze. "I've been here nearly three months now."

"Yes."

"You asked me and I came without question. I've never asked to go free."

A sense of dread filled McFarland. "What are you saying?"

"John, please, I want to go home."

Chapter Nine

I won't let you go," McFarland answered thickly.

Judy closed her eyes to the bittersweet pain. "I haven't amused you enough?" At his blank stare, she continued. "That was the reason you brought me to the island, or so you claimed."

"That has nothing to do with it."

"Then what does?"

McFarland's control was slipping and rather than argue, he reached for his pen and scribbled instructions across the top of a sheet. If he ignored her, maybe she would forget her request and drop the entire matter.

"John," she said softly. "I'm not going away until you answer me."

"I've already said everything I intend to. The subject is closed."

"The subject is standing in front of you demanding an answer!"

"You're my guest."

"But you won't allow me to leave."

A strained, heavy silence fell between them. Judy's breathing was fast and shallow. Her throat burned as she struggled to hold back her emotions.

"John, please."

"You are my guest."

"I may leave?"

"*No!*" His rage was palpable. He didn't know why,

after all these weeks, she would ask him to release her. His heart felt like a stone in his chest.

The ugly silence returned.

When Judy spoke again, her voice was incredibly soft, yet tortured. "Then I'm your prisoner."

She turned and left him, feeling as though she were living out her worst nightmare. She dared not look back; the tears nearly blinded her as she stepped out of his office.

McFarland watched her go, overcome by an unidentifiable, raw emotion. She claimed to be his prisoner, but there were chains that bound him just as strongly. She'd come to him and within a matter of weeks had altered the course of his life. He couldn't afford to lose Judy—she was his sunshine, his joy. She'd brought summer to the dark winter of his existence. Dear God, how could he ever let her go?

Judy returned to her suite. Dark clouds weighted her heart. She'd been happy with John and the island life. Everything had been good—until she had seen the cell. Now she stood in front of her own set of bars, her hands gripping the steel of her gilded cage. Like the bird wildly seeking escape, her wings were frantically beating, seeking freedom.

When her eyes were empty of tears, she took her brother's letter and withdrew it from the envelope. For the third time, she read it. Every word was a more painful form of torture. Things she'd taken for granted returned to haunt her. Bently and the funny way he had of speaking out of the corner of his mouth; the dining-room chairs that were a family heritage; the Priscilla drapes that hung over her bedroom windows.

Her beloved brother was getting married. Some of the weight lifted from her heart as she thought of David as a husband and someday a father. Marie would make him a good wife. His excitement and joy were evident in the letter. She could almost see him with his eyes sparkling and his arm around Marie's shoulder. How Judy wished she could be with him to share in this special moment.

At noon, although she had no appetite, Judy left her rooms and paused just inside the dining room. John was waiting for her, standing at his end of the table, his hands braced against the back of his chair.

"Are you feeling better?" he asked cordially.

"No." She dropped her gaze to the table. A small, beautifully wrapped gift rested beside her water glass. She raised questioning eyes to John, unsure of what to make of this.

"Go ahead and open it."

She wanted to tell him that she wouldn't accept any more gifts. He couldn't buy her as he'd done everything else in his life. She wasn't for sale. The only thing she sought from John McFarland was the freedom to return home, and he wouldn't allow that.

Dutifully, she sat down and peeled away the paper. Inside was a diamond bracelet of such elegance and beauty that her breath caught in her lungs. "It's beautiful."

John looked exceedingly pleased. "I was saving it for just the right moment."

Judy gently closed the velvet box and set it aside. "Why now? Did you want to prove that my shackles are indeed jewel-encrusted? You needn't have bothered, John. I've always known that."

His face convulsed and, as he stared at her, his eyes grew dark and hot.

Neither spoke another word during their meal, and when Judy left the dining room, she pointedly left the bracelet behind.

A week passed, the longest, most difficult week of Judy's life. She didn't ask John to release her again, but her desire to leave the island hung between them at every meeting. Although she avoided him, he seemed to create excuses to be with her. He chatted easily, telling her little things, pretending nothing had changed. Judy wasn't that good an actress; she spoke only when he directed a question to her. Although she strove to remain distant and aloof, it was difficult.

To work out her frustration, she rode long hours across the island. The sweltering heat of late summer was oppressive. One afternoon toward dusk, she changed from her riding clothes into her swimming suit.

The pool was blissfully cool when she dove in. She hoped the refreshing water would help alleviate the discomfort of the merciless sun and her own restlessness. She swam lazy laps, drawing comfort from the effort of mundane exercise.

She hadn't been in the water ten minutes when John joined her. As he approached the pool, Judy swam to the shallow end, stood up and shakily brushed the wet hair from her face. She defied him with her eyes, demanding that he leave and give her some privacy.

He ignored her silent pleas and jumped into the pool. At first he did little more than laps. Somewhat relieved, Judy continued her exercise. When he suddenly appeared beside her, it was a surprise.

"Remember the last time we were in the water together?" he asked, his voice husky and low.

In an effort to get away from him, Judy swam to the deep end and treaded water. She remembered that afternoon on the beach all too well; he'd held her in his arms while the rolling surf plunged them underwater. He had kissed her and held her body close to his as the powerful surf had tossed them about.

Now his presence trapped her. She refused to meet his commanding look.

"You remember, don't you?" He demanded an answer.

"Yes," she cried, and swallowed hard.

His face tightened and he lowered his voice, each syllable more seductive than the last. "So do I, Judy. I remember the way you slid your arms around my neck and buried your face in my chest."

She shook her head in silent denial.

"You trembled when I kissed you and you clung to

me as though I were your life. I remember every-thing. You tasted of sunshine and honey."

Judy closed her eyes. "And salt," she whispered involuntarily. "You claimed I tasted like salt."

"That, too."

"Don't." She desperately wanted him to leave her and pleaded in a hoarse whisper for him to do exactly that.

"I'm not going." He noted that her eyes were overly bright and that she was struggling to hold back the tears. "I miss you. I want things to go back to the way they were."

Her chin rose and the blood drained from her face. "It can't," she cried, her mouth trembling. "It never can again."

As much as he tried, McFarland couldn't under-stand what had changed. Why had she all of a sudden come to him and asked to return to New York? He had tried—God knew he'd tried—to understand, but she'd made it impossible. In a week, she hadn't spoken more than a few times to him. He'd attempted to draw her out, to discover what was troubling her. All she did was look at him with her large, soulful eyes as though she would burst into tears at any moment. After a week, he was quickly losing his patience.

"Why can't it be the same?" he asked.

"I'm your prisoner."

"You aren't," he shouted.

"You brought me here as an amusement."

"You won't let her off the island even to attend her brother's wedding?"

"No."

"But, sir . . ."

"That will be all, Avery."

McFarland's assistant squared his shoulders and paused as though gathering his courage before speaking.

"Listen, Avery," McFarland barked, unwilling to listen to anyone's opinion regarding Judy. His mind was set. "Feel free to submit your resignation. Only next time I may not be so willing to give it back when you change your mind."

That evening, McFarland sat alone in the library. Over the years since he'd been on the island, he'd spent countless nights in this room. Now it felt as cold and unwelcoming as an unmarked grave. When he couldn't tolerate it any longer, he rose and stepped outside, heading toward the stables. A beer with Sam would ease his mind. He was halfway there when he saw Judy, silhouetted in the moonlight, sitting on the patio by the pool. Her head was slightly bowed, the soft folds of her summer dress pleated evenly around her. The pale light of the moon shone like a halo for the angel she was. Her soft gentleness had never been more apparent.

The scene affected him more than all her pleas. He remembered standing on the ridge and watching her play with the island children on the beach below. He

"In the beginning, perhaps, but that's all changed."

"But it hasn't," she said flatly. "Nothing has. I'm your pawn."

"But you were happy."

She flinched at the truth. "Yes, for a time I was."

"What changed?"

"The walls," she said in a tormented voice. "I could see the walls closing in around me."

McFarland hadn't a clue as to what she was talking about. Walls? What walls? She had more freedom now than she recognized. She ruled his heart; he was hers to do with as she wished.

"Judy," he said, trapping her against the bright blue tile of the pool. His face was only inches from hers. "You're talking nonsense."

"To you, maybe . . . you don't understand."

"I only understand this," he said, weaving his fingers into her wet hair. He kissed her then, pressing his body against her own as he hungrily claimed her mouth, branding her as his.

Judy fought him, bunching her fists and hitting him where she could. Her frantic blows didn't faze him and, with a whimper, she pressed her hands against his broad chest and pushed with all her might.

"Don't fight me," he moaned, holding her tighter. He rubbed his mouth seductively over hers, lightly teasing her, testing her. "It was good with us. You can't have forgotten how good."

"Yes, I remember," she wept. Instinctively, her body arched toward him and she slipped her arms tightly around his neck. She was trembling when he kissed her again and she arched intimately against him. Her mouth opened eagerly to him, giving him everything he wanted. His senses reeled and he nearly lost his grip on the pool's edge.

"I can't let you go," he whispered, and kissed her gently, slowly, again and again until she was weak and clinging in his arms. His body burned with need for her. Raising his head, he looked into her eyes. "I'll give you anything."

Tears scorched a trail down her face. "I only want one thing."

Knowing what she was about to say, McFarland closed his eyes to the pain that lacerated his heart.

"I want my freedom," she sobbed. Her shoulders shook uncontrollably as she climbed out of the pool. "I want to go home."

Guilt tore at him. He could deal with anything but her pain. Judy was using his twisted conscience against him and in that moment, McFarland was convinced he hated her.

Then, seeing her tear-streaked face as she reached for the towel and ran from him, McFarland realized something more—he hated himself twice as much.

Her tears didn't abate, even when Judy returned to her room. The power John had to bend her will to his own shook her to the core of her being. How easily he had manipulated her. His kisses were more potent than her desire to return to her family. Within minutes she had become weak, willing to give him anything he desired.

160

When McFarland returned to his office, his mood was dark. He was short-tempered with anyone who had the misfortune of being within earshot. It was as though he wanted to punish the world for trying to take the only woman he'd ever cared about from him.

"Mr. McFarland," Avery said, late that same afternoon. He stood just inside the office, not daring to approach his employer's desk.

"What is it?" McFarland barked. "I haven't got all day."

"It's Miss Lovin, sir."

The pencil McFarland was holding snapped in half. "She's staying, Avery, and there's not a damn thing you can say that will change my mind."

"But, sir . . ."

"In time, she'll accept matters as they are."

"But her family . . ."

"What about them?"

"They've personally appealed for your mercy. It seems the Lovin boy is getting married and requests his sister's presence at the wedding."

"They appealed for mercy! I hope you told them I have none." McFarland shuffled through some papers, paying unnecessary attention to them.

"The family's requesting some indication of when you plan to release Miss Lovin. The wedding can be delayed at . . . at your convenience."

"Mine," he snickered loudly. "I hope you told them I have no plans of releasing her."

161

recalled how her eyes would light up just before his mouth met hers; he recalled how she clung to him. With vivid clarity, he remembered the fall from the horse's back and how he would have given everything he had owned not to see her hurt or taken from him. Now, although she wasn't permanently injured, he was losing her.

His presence must have disturbed her, because she turned and her eyes found his. McFarland's stomach knotted at the doubt and uncertainty he saw in her gaze. With everything that was in him, he yearned to ease her pain, but in doing so he would only increase his own. He needed her now. The beast who had once claimed he needed no one was dependent upon a mere woman.

The sudden thunder and lightning barely registered in McFarland's mind. The drenching rain soaked him in minutes, and still he didn't move.

Judy came to him, her gaze concerned.

"Go inside," he rasped.

Her face was bloodless and strained. "Not without you."

He nearly laughed at her concern. It shouldn't matter to her what became of him; she was the one who wanted to walk out of his life.

"John." She urged him again a moment later.

"I find your solicitude a little short of amusing." The flatness of his voice sent a chill through her veins. Judy hesitated.

He noted then that she was as drenched as he. "Go

inside," he murmured. "I'll be in after a few minutes."

"If you stay out here, you'll catch a chill."

Raw emotion fueled his anger and he shouted loudly enough to be heard over the furious clap of thunder. "Leave me!"

Her eyes welled with tears.

McFarland couldn't bear to see her cry. He stepped close and cupped her sweet face. His heart ached with all the emotion he felt for her. He could make her stay, force her to live on the island and ignore her desire to leave. In time she would forget her family, accept her position on St. Steven's and in his life. He would give her everything a woman would possibly want; everything he owned would be hers.

In that moment, McFarland knew that everything he possessed, all his wealth, all that he was, would never be enough for Judy. He dropped his hands and turned toward the house.

When they reached the front door, John opened it for her. Judy paused and looked up at him. If she were unhappy, she was barely upset compared to the misery she witnessed in his eyes.

"John," she whispered brokenly. Even now his unhappiness greatly affected her. Even now she loved him. "I . . ."

His face tightened as a dark mask descended over his features, a mask she recognized readily. He'd worn it often the first weeks after her arrival. She had forgotten how cold and cruel he could look, how ruthless he could be.

"Don't say it," he interrupted harshly. "Don't say one damn thing. Not a word." He turned and abruptly left her standing alone. Without looking back once, he moved out of the foyer.

Princess was saddled and ready for Judy early the next morning. She hadn't slept well and looked forward to the rigorous exercise.

"Morning, Sam," she said, without much enthusiasm.

The groom ignored her, cupping a stallion's hoof in his lap and running a file across the underside.

"Sam?"

"Morning," he grumbled, not looking at her.

"Is something wrong?" Sam had been her ally and friend from the first.

"Wrong? he repeated. "What could be wrong?"

"I don't know."

"For nearly two weeks now this place has been like a battlefield."

Judy opened her mouth to deny it.

"But does ol' Sam question it? No." He answered his own inquiry and raised his head to glare at her. "I figured whatever was wrong would right itself in time. Looks like I was wrong."

"I wish it were that simple," Judy murmured, stroking Princess's neck.

Sam continued to run the file back and forth across

the stallion's hoof. "McFarland bites my head off and you walk around here looking like you spent half the night crying your eyes out. You get any paler and someone could mistake you for a ghost!"

Judy raised her hands to her cheeks, embarrassed.

Sam lowered the stallion's leg to the ground and slowly straightened. "McFarland's been shouting at you again?"

"No."

"Has he been unfair?"

"That's not what this is about."

"Did he get after you for something you didn't do?"

"No."

Hands on his hips, Sam took a step toward her. "Do you love him or not?"

Judy felt the blood rush through her veins.

"Well?" he demanded.

"Yes," she answered, her voice shaking uncontrollably.

"I thought so."

She pushed the hair out of her face. "Loving someone doesn't make everything right."

"Then do whatever it is you have to do to make it that way."

Judy swallowed down the hard lump that had formed in her throat. Sam made everything sound so uncomplicated.

"For heaven's sake, woman, put an end to this infernal bickering. And do it soon, while there's still a man or woman who's willing to remain in McFarland's employ."

Judy rode for hours. When she returned, a maid announced that McFarland wished to see her at her earliest convenience. With her heart pounding, Judy rushed up the stairs for a quick shower.

By the time she appeared in John's office Avery looked greatly relieved to see her.

"You're to go right in," he instructed.

"Thank you, Avery," she said as he opened the door for her.

John was writing, his head bent, and although she was fairly certain he knew she was there, he chose to ignore her.

After the longest minute of her life, he raised his gaze to hers and gestured for her to take a seat. His look was cool and distant.

Judy shivered as she sat down. "I've been in communication with New York this morning," he said evenly.

She nodded, not knowing exactly what he was leading up to. He could be referring to her family, but he hadn't said as much.

"The launch will leave the island at five tomorrow morning. However, the copter is at your disposal."

Judy blinked. "Are you saying I'm free to leave?"

"That's exactly what I'm saying."

It took a minute for the full realization to hit Judy. She sighed as the great burden was lifted from her shoulders. "John . . ."

He ignored her. "From what I understand, you'll be home in plenty of time for your brother's wedding."

Her smile was tremulous. "Thank you."

He nodded abruptly. "Is tomorrow soon enough, or would you prefer to leave now?"

"Tomorrow is fine."

He returned to his paperwork.

"John . . ."

"If you'll excuse me, I have work to do," he said pointedly.

The icy harshness in his voice was a slap in the face. Judy stood, clasping her fingers tightly in front of her. "I'll never forget you, John McFarland, or this island."

He continued with his work as though she hadn't spoken.

"If I don't see you again . . ."

John glanced at his watch and while she was speaking, reached for his phone and punched out a number.

Judy blinked back stinging tears of anger and embarrassment.

"Goodbye, John," she said softly, and with great dignity, turned and left his office.

That evening Judy ate alone. The dining-room table had never seemed so big or the room so empty. She'd spent the afternoon preparing for her departure. Her suitcase was packed, her room bare of the items that had marked it as hers. She'd visited the children one last time and had stopped at the stables to feed Princess and Midnight. Sam had grumbled disapprovingly when he heard she was leaving and when she hugged him goodbye, the gruff old man's eyes glistened.

"I didn't think you'd fix things up this way," he barked.

After all the excitement, Judy had expected to sleep that evening. To her surprise, she couldn't.

At midnight, she silently made her way down the stairs for a glass of milk. The light from under the library door surprised her. She cracked it open to investigate and found John sitting at the oak desk, a half-full whiskey bottle in one hand and a shot glass in the other.

He raised his gaze to study her when she entered the room. His eyes widened in disbelief, then narrowed. "What are you doing here?"

The words were slurred and barely discernible. Judy shook her head, hardly able to believe what she was seeing. In all the weeks that she'd been on the island, John had never abused alcohol. "You're drunk."

He lifted the bottle in mocking salute. "You're damn right I am."

"Oh, John." She nervously tucked her hair behind her ear, feeling wretched.

"You think too highly of yourself if you believe I did this because you're leaving."

"I . . ."

He refilled his glass, the whiskey sloshing over the sides of the glass. He downed the contents in one swallow and glared at her maliciously. "You were a damn nuisance."

Judy swallowed a heated response.

"I would have done well to be rid of you weeks ago."

Ten excellent excuses to turn and walk away presented themselves. Judy ignored each one. For some perverse reason she wanted to hear what he had to say.

"You're such a damn goody-goody."

She clasped her fingers more tightly together.

Again he filled the shot glass. "I could have had you several different times. You know that, don't you? God knows, you were willing enough." His eyes challenged her to defy him. "But I didn't take what you so generously offered me." His short laugh lacked humor. He bent forward and glared at her. "You know why? I like my women hot and spicy. You're sweet, but you'd soon grow tasteless."

Judy felt as though her face were red enough to guide lost ships into harbor. Each word was a lash across her tender back, salt to the wound, alcohol poured over the festering sore.

His eyes grew cold as he glared at her. He took a drink straight from the bottle. "Why are you still standing there?"

Judy couldn't answer him. She shook her head and wiped the moisture from her face.

"Get out," he roared. "Out of my house! Out of my life!"

A part of Judy yearned to wrap her arms around him and absorb his anger. The battle raged within her.

"Go on," he shouted forcefully. "Get out of here before I do something we'll both regret."

"Goodbye, John," she whispered tightly. She closed the massive doors when she left and flinched at the unexpected sound of breaking glass.

"Goodbye, Beauty."

The words were so faint that Judy wasn't convinced she had heard them.

Judy sat in her room, waiting for the sun to rise. She hadn't slept after the confrontation in the library; she hadn't even tried.

At four, the maid came to wake her and was surprised to find her already up. "Mr. Andersen will escort you to the dock," the girl informed her.

"Thank you."

Avery was waiting for Judy at the bottom of the stairs. He took the lone suitcase from her hand and gave her a sympathetic look. Judy paused and glanced in the direction of the library.

"Take care of him for me, will you?" she asked.

Avery cleared his throat and looked doubtful. "I'll do my best."

The launch was waiting for them at the dock. Judy hugged John's assistant and Sam, who arrived at the last minute, looking flustered and upset.

Only when the boat had sped away did Judy dare to glance back to the island. In the distance she saw a third figure standing separate from the others.

John McFarland watched the only woman he had ever loved vanish from his life. In releasing her, he had committed the ultimate sacrifice. It was probably the only completely unselfish deed of his lonely life.

Chapter Ten

The sound was what astonished Judy most. Street noise: buses, taxis, traffic, shouts, raised voices, laughter, televisions, radios. The clamor wasn't as irritating as it was distracting. The island had taught her to appreciate the wonders of silence.

But this was Manhattan, not St. Steven's Island, Judy had to repeatedly remind herself. The first few days following her arrival home, she'd felt as though she had returned to another planet. The life that had once been familiar and comfortable felt strangely out of sync and appallingly loud. In time, she realized, she would adjust, just as she had adapted to life on the island.

"It's McFarland, isn't it?" her father asked her over breakfast the first week she was home.

"John?"

Charles Lovin's features were tight with anxiety. Their months apart had taken their toll on the elder Lovin. It showed in the way his eyes followed her, his gaze sad and greatly troubled. "McFarland treated you abominably, didn't he?"

"Of course not," Judy answered, dismissing her father's fears with a generous smile. "John McFarland was the perfect gentleman."

"From the beginning?"

Judy lowered her gaze to her plate as an unexpected twinge of loneliness brought tears to her eyes. "In his own way, yes. He's an unusual person."

"You think I don't know that? I died a thousand deaths worrying about you alone on that island with that . . . that animal."

"I wasn't alone with John and, Father, really, he isn't a beast."

Charles Lovin's instant denial faded quickly in Judy's ears. She pretended to be listening while her father listed John's many faults in a loud, haranguing voice. Her thoughts were a thousand miles away on a Caribbean island where orchids grew in abundance and children laughed and a man ruled his own kingdom.

"Judy, are you listening to me? Judy?"

"I'm sorry," she said contritely, looking to her father. "What was it you were saying?"

Father and son exchanged meaningful glances.

"I'm sure you can appreciate that Dad and I were concerned about you," David said, studying his sister thoughtfully.

"Naturally, I would have been worried myself had the circumstances been reversed," Judy murmured, feeling wretched. She wanted to defend John, but both her father and her brother were filled with bitterness toward him.

"He never spoke to us personally," David continued. "I can't begin to tell you how frustrated Dad and I were. We must have contacted McFarland a hundred times and never got past that harebrained assistant of his. By the way, what's this Andersen fellow like?"

"Avery?"

"Yes. I tell you, he's an expert at sidestepping questions. No matter how much Dad and I hounded him, we never could get a straight answer."

At the memory of Avery Andersen, Judy brightened and spent the next five minutes describing John's assistant. "He really is a funny little man. So polite and . . ."

"Polite!" Her father nearly choked on his coffee. "The next thing I know you'll be telling me McFarland is a saint."

Judy blushed at the memory of all the times he could have made love to her, and hadn't. "In some ways he was a saint."

Her announcement was followed by a stunned silence.

"Any man who pulls the kind of stunts John McFarland does will burn in hell," Charles Lovin stated emphatically.

"Father!"

"I mean it. That man is a demon."

Judy pushed her plate aside and valiantly managed not to defend John. "And just what did he do that was so terrible?"

"Why, he . . . he nearly destroyed our business."

"It's thriving now; you told me so yourself."

"Now!" The elder Lovin spat. "But McFarland drove us to the brink of disaster, then took delight in toying with us."

"He told me once that he held you in high regard," Judy informed him.

"Then Lord help us if he ever covets my friendship!"

With great difficulty, Judy kept her own counsel. Neither her father nor her brother could understand John the way she did. Given their position, she would probably feel differently, but that didn't change her opinion of him, her love for him.

"Does he do this sort of thing often?" David asked, as he sliced into his ham.

Judy blinked, not understanding.

"Were there other women on the island?" he elaborated.

"A few. But I was the only one he . . ." She paused and searched for the right word.

"You were the only woman he blackmailed into coming?" her father finished for her.

"The only one he sent for," Judy corrected calmly.

"That man is a menace to society," Charles muttered angrily as he sipped his coffee.

Judy couldn't tolerate their insults any longer. She sighed and shook her head. "I hate to disappoint you both, but John McFarland is kind and good. He treated me with the utmost respect the entire time I was on the island."

"He held you like a prisoner of war."

"He released me when I asked," she told them, stretching the truth only a bit.

"He did?"

"Of course." She dabbed the corner of her mouth with her napkin, ignoring the way both family members were staring at her with their mouths gaping open.

"He held you for three months, Judy," David said, watching her keenly. "You mean to say that in all that time you never asked to leave?"

"That's right."

Again father and son exchanged looks.

"I don't expect you to understand," she told them lamely. "The island is a tropical paradise. I didn't think to ask to leave until . . . until the end."

The dining room grew silent.

Her father hugged Judy before she left the room. "It's good to have you home, Beauty."

"It's good to be home."

In her bedroom, Judy ran her fingers over the brocade-covered headboard and experienced none of the homecoming sensations she'd expected. She loved this room; it was a part of her youth, a part of her existence before she had met John McFarland.

Sitting on her mattress now, Judy experienced a poignant sense of loss. She'd changed on the island, blossomed. John had taught her what it was to be a woman and no matter how much she would have wished it, she couldn't go back to being the frightened girl who had left New York destined for a Caribbean island.

A letdown was only natural, Judy tried to reason with herself. When she'd been on the island, home had seemed ideal. Everything was perfect in New York. There were no problems, no difficulties, no heartache. To her dismay, she was learning that reality falls far short of memory.

A polite knock at her door diverted her attention from her troubled thoughts. "Come in."

Marie Ashley, David's fiancé, walked into the room. "Are you ready?"

"I've been ready for weeks," Judy said, rising from the bed. She slipped on a pair of comfortable shoes. "I plan to shop till I drop."

"Me, too," Marie said, her eyes shining. "David and I need so many things. Oh, Judy, we're going to be so happy." She hugged her arms around her middle and sighed with ecstasy. "Did he tell you that I broke into tears when he proposed? I couldn't even answer him. Poor David, I'm sure he didn't know what to make of me, blubbering and carrying on like that."

"I imagine he got the message when you threw your arms around his neck and started kissing him."

Marie's hands flew to her hips. "He told you!"

"Ten times the first day I was home," Judy informed her cheerfully. "I don't know who is more excited, you or my brother."

"Me," Marie said unequivocally.

Laughing, the two hurried down the stairs to the sports car Marie had parked out front.

The day was a busy one. True to their word, both women shopped until their feet ached and they couldn't carry another package. They ended up back at the Lovin family home, bringing take-out Chinese food with them.

Judy deposited her shopping bags in the polished entryway. "Bently," she called, "we're home."

A quick grin cracked the butler's stiff facade as he regarded the pair of them. He already treated Marie like a family member. "Several wedding gifts arrived this afternoon," he informed them primly.

"Here?" Marie asked, surprised.

"I can assure you, Miss Ashley, I did not haul them from your family's home."

"Where are they, Bently?" Judy asked, sharing a smile with Marie.

"I placed them in the library."

"Come on," Marie said eagerly, "let's go check out the loot."

Judy followed her soon-to-be sister-in-law into the book-lined room.

"I took the liberty of unwrapping them for you," Bently said.

Both Judy and Marie paused in the doorway and gasped at the rich display of paintings and sculptures. The room went still and Judy's hand flew to her heart. Each piece was lovingly familiar; they were the items her father had sold in a desperate attempt to save the shipping line. The ones he had surrendered piece by piece, prolonging the agony.

"All this?" Marie gasped. "Who? Who would possibly give us so much?"

Judy knew the answer even before Bently spoke. "The card says John McFarland."

Judy's eyes drifted shut. John, her John.

"Why, he's the man . . ." Marie stopped short. "Judy?" Her voice was low and hesitant. "Are you all right?"

Judy forced her eyes open. "Of course. Why shouldn't I be?"

"You look like you're about to faint."

"It's from lack of nourishment," Judy explained, her voice shaking. "You dragged me through half the department stores in Manhattan and didn't feed me lunch. What do you expect?"

"I want you to tell me everything. Now sit down." Judy followed the order because she wasn't convinced she could remain upright for much longer. "Bently, bring us some coffee."

"Right away, Miss Ashley."

Despite her misery, Judy smiled, finding a new respect for her brother's fiancé. "I swear, within a year you'll be the one running the family business."

"I'll have my hands full managing David," Marie returned matter-of-factly.

The coffee arrived and Marie poured, handing Judy the first cup. "You don't need to say much," she began gently. "It's obvious to me that you love him."

Judy dropped her gaze. "I do. Unfortunately, my family hates him. They think he's some kind of monster."

179

"But you know better?"

"I do, Marie. He frightened me in the beginning; he can be terrifying. Believe me, I know he's arrogant and stubborn, but as the weeks passed, I discovered that underneath he was a man like every other man. One with hurts and doubts and fears. I learned how kind and generous he can be."

"But, Judy, he forced you to live on that island."

"It's beautiful there. Paradise."

"David and your father were convinced he was mistreating you."

"Never. Not intentionally. Once I had an accident— my fault, actually, although John seemed to blame himself and . . ."

Marie gasped.

"I didn't let my family know," Judy explained patiently. "They would have only worried and I couldn't see any point in increasing their anxiety."

"What happened?"

"I fell—it doesn't matter. What is important is that John was so wonderful to me. I've never seen anyone more concerned. He spent hours taking care of me. I think he slept in my room for at least two nights. Every time I woke up, he was there. I . . . I didn't know any man could be so gentle."

Marie smiled faintly. "What are you planning to do now?"

Judy held the coffee cup in both hands. "I . . . don't know."

"Do you want to go back to the island?"

Judy hung her head and whispered. "Yes. Nothing's the same without John. I loved St. Steven's, but more importantly I love John."

"Oh, Judy, your father . . ."

"I know." She managed to keep her voice steady. "I think he'd rather die than see me go back to the island. John will always be the beast in his eyes."

"Give him time," Marie suggested softly. "Look what happened with David and me."

Judy wasn't sure she understood. "I know that David hasn't seen anyone but you for a couple of years."

"Five years, Judy, I waited five long years for that man."

Judy had no idea the romance between them had been brewing all that time.

"With all the financial problems with the business, David told me it could be years before he saw his way clear to marry me or anyone. He told me it was useless for me to wait."

"How painful for you."

"Oh, it gets worse. He broke off our relationship and suggested I marry someone else. When I refused, he insisted that I start seeing other men. He made a point of introducing me to his friends and when that didn't work . . ." She hedged, and her eyes grew dull with pain.

"What happened?" Judy asked gently.

"I wouldn't give up on him. I loved him too much. If he didn't want to marry me, then I was destined to die an old maid. There's never been anyone else for me. Only David."

"What did he do?"

Marie's smile revealed a great sadness. "He said some cruel things to me in an effort to keep me from—what he called—wasting my life."

Judy recalled her last night on the island and the horrible things John had said to her. He loved her; she was sure of it. But he had never asked her to stay, never told her he loved her. Still, she knew he loved her, just as he must have known.

"Of course, all his angry insults didn't work," Marie continued. "I knew what he was doing. He couldn't have gotten rid of me to save his soul."

"I take it he tried."

Marie's mouth quivered. "Oh, yes, for months. Inventive schemes, too, I might add, but I'm more stubborn than he took into account."

Judy gripped her friend's hand. "I hope he appreciates how lucky he is."

"Are you kidding? I plan to remind him every day for the next fifty years. Now," she said forcefully, sucking in a huge breath. "It's your turn, Judy Lovin, to prove to a man that you mean business."

Judy's gaze rested on their clasped hands. "The night before I left the island, I found John . . . drinking. He told me he was glad to see me go."

"What did you say?"

"Nothing."

"Good."

"Good?"

"Right. He didn't mean it."

"I know. He was hurting."

Marie smiled then, knowingly. "The guilt is probably driving him crazy about now."

Judy studied her brother's fiancé. "What makes you say that?"

Marie gestured with her hand toward the array of wedding gifts that filled the library. "Look around you, Judy Lovin."

"But . . ."

"No buts, girl," Marie interrupted. "You're going back to the island. And when you do he'll so happy to see you there won't be a single doubt."

Judy went pale.

"It's what you want, isn't it?"

"Yes, but Father and David . . ."

"Just who are you planning to spend the rest of your life with, anyway? Do you presume to believe they'll appreciate your sacrifice? Do you think my family was overjoyed with me hanging around year after year?" Marie asked. "Good grief, no! They were convinced that unless I married David, I was going to become a permanent fixture in the old homestead."

Judy laughed, despite her misery.

"My dad was so desperate to get rid of me that he started bringing home strangers off the streets to introduce to his spinster daughter. I'm telling you, between David and my father, I turned down two neurosurgeons, a dentist, three attorneys and a construction tycoon."

The thought was so ridiculous that Judy couldn't stop laughing. Soon Marie joined her and the two kept it up until their sides hurt and tears rolled down their faces.

That one talk with her future sister-in-law gave Judy all the fortitude she needed to face an army of Charles Lovins. She chose her moment well—the reception following David and Marie's wedding.

"Father," she said, standing beside him in the receiving line. "I have something to tell you."

He shook hands with a family friend before turning his attention to his daughter. "Yes, Beauty."

"I love John McFarland."

She expected a bellow of outrage, anger . . . something other than his acceptance and love. "I suspected as much. Are you going back to him?"

Tears brimmed in Judy's eyes. "Yes."

"When?" His own voice sounded chocked.

"Soon."

"He'll marry you?"

Judy chuckled and winked at her sister-in-law. "He'd better."

Charles Lovin arched thick eyebrows. "Why's that?"

"I'm not taking no for an answer. Marie and I have a bet on which one of us is going to present you with your first grandchild."

The older man's eyes sparkled with unshed tears at the prospect. "Then what are you doing sticking around here?" He turned her in his arms and hugged her fiercely. "Be very, very happy."

"I know I will. You'll come visit?"

"If he'll allow it."

Her arms tightened around him. "He will, I promise."

The launch slowed to a crawl as it approached the dock of St. Steven's Island. Two formidable security guards were waiting to intercept the unannounced intruders.

"Miss Lovin?"

"Hello, Wilson," Judy said, handing him her luggage. "Is Mr. McFarland available?"

The guard looked uncertain. "I believe he is. Does he know you're coming?"

"No."

He winced at that, but didn't hesitate to help her climb out of the boat.

"Will you see to it that my things are delivered to my room?" Judy asked.

"Right away."

"Thank you, Wilson."

By the time Judy arrived at the house, there was a small army of McFarland employees following her, all talking excitedly.

Sam arrived, breathless from the stables. "Hot dog," he cried and slapped his knee. "It's about time you got here."

"I was only gone two weeks."

"That's about thirteen days too long!"

"How has he been?"

Sam shook his head. "Meaner than a saddle sore."

Judy glanced around to note that several of the other employees were nodding their heads, agreeing with Sam's assessment.

"He's fired me three times in the last week alone," Wilson volunteered.

"*Moi aussi,*" the chef added, ceremoniously crossing his arms over his chest and pointing his nose toward the sky, greatly insulted. "He had zee nerve to suggest I return to cooking school."

"Everything will be better now that Miss Lovin's back," Sam assured the irate staff. "Next time you leave, though," the groom warned Judy, "we'll all be on that boat with you."

"I won't be leaving," she told them confidently.

A small cheer arose and when Judy entered the house, she was met with a red-faced Avery.

"Miss Lovin!" He looked stunned, flustered, then greatly relieved. "Oh, thank God you're back."

"Where is he?" she asked, resisting the urge to hug her friend.

"The library." He pointed in the direction of the closed doors as though he'd expected her to have forgotten. "I tried to take care of him like you wanted," Avery said, his words coming out in a rush. "Only, Mr. McFarland, well, he didn't exactly take kindly to my solicitude."

186

"I can imagine," Judy said, grateful for such loyal friends.

Gathering her courage, she stood in front of the library doors. She found it fitting that he would be there. The last time she had confronted him had been in the paneled, book-lined room. Only this time, she planned to do all the talking.

She didn't knock, but gently opened the doors and stepped inside.

"I said I wasn't to be disturbed," John shouted.

Judy's heart constricted at the sight he made, hunched behind a desk. He looked hard, his blue eyes void of any emotion except anger and regret. She noted the lines of fatigue around his eyes and the flatness of his hard mouth.

"John, it's me," she said softly, loving him so much that only her strong will prevented her from walking into his arms.

His head snapped up. His eyes went wide with questioning disbelief and he half rose from his chair. "Beauty." He froze as though he couldn't decide what to do.

"Don't, John."

"Don't?" he repeated, puzzled.

"Don't ask me to leave. I won't, you know."

McFarland heard the catch in her voice and sank back into the leather chair. How well she knew him; the words had dangled on the tip of his tongue to demand that she march back where she came from. It wasn't what he wanted, but he had to protect her from himself.

Judy moved farther into the room. "David's wedding was beautiful, and ours is going to be just as special."

"Ours?" he mocked.

"Yes, ours! You're marrying me, John McFarland."

"You're sure as hell taking a lot for granted."

"Perhaps."

"Judy, no." He wiped his hand over his face, thinking this all could be a dream. It wasn't. "Don't do this. You're making sending you away damn difficult."

She boldly met his glare. "I plan on making it impossible."

He closed his eyes and said nothing for the longest moment. "Judy, there's someone better for you in New York. Some man who will give you the kind of life you deserve. Some man your father will approve of. He's right—I am a beast."

She planted her hands on his desktop, remembering everything Marie had gone through for David. "I only want you."

"Forcing you to live on the island was a mistake." His face revealed nothing, but she felt the powerful undertow of his emotions.

"It's right for me to love you, John."

He flinched as though she'd struck him.

"I'm not good enough for you," he told her in a hard, implacable voice. "The things I did to your family . . . the things I did to you."

"Coming to this island was right for me. You're

right for me. I love you. All I ask is that you love me in return."

Again he flinched, and his jaw tightened. He reached out and gently stroked her cheek. "I've loved you from the moment you showed me how you'd tamed Midnight."

Her gaze holding his, Judy walked around the desk. McFarland stood.

She slipped her arms around his neck and leaned her weight into him. "Oh, John, life isn't right without you. I had to leave you to learn that there's no one for me anyplace else but right here."

"Judy." He groaned and sought her mouth with a hunger that had been fed with self-hatred and weeks of loneliness. His fingers plowed through her hair as he slanted his mouth over hers. He kissed her again and again, as though it would take a hundred years to make up for the two weeks without her.

"I live in a tropical paradise and it was winter without you," he breathed into her hair.

"It's summer now," she answered, her eyes glistening.

"Yes," he said, his voice raw. His hand was gentle on her hair. "I love you, Beauty. God knows why you want to marry a beast."

"I have my reasons," she said as she lovingly pushed him back into his chair. "There's a small wager I need to tell you about."

"Oh?" He pulled her into his lap and she leaned forward and whispered it in his ear.

The sound of McFarland's laughter drifted through the library doors and the seven who had gathered there sighed contentedly.

Winter had left St. Steven's never to return.

From that moment, the islanders liked to tell how the Beast was gone forever.

Beauty had tamed him.